Rain Falling On Bells

Fragments Of Truths [3rd Ed

To Order: AMAZON BOOKS

Publisher's Note: This is a work of fiction. Names, characters, places, and incidents are a product of the author's imagination. Locales and public names are sometimes used for atmospheric purposes. Any resemblance to actual people, living or dead, or to businesses, companies, events, institutions, or locales is completely coincidental.

All Biblical verses used are from the King James Version [KJV] of the Bible.

Special discounts may be available on quantity purchases.

Rain Falling On Bells: Fragments Of Truths/ *Allen James Gourley.*

Special Heartfelt Thanks:
Pre-Editing: Danielle E., Maggie M., Susie G. and Dana G.
2nd Edit: Mr. Leonard Cherico

Author's Original Manuscript

ISBN: 9781726721493

II

Dedication

GOD ALMIGHTY has blessed me with the most wonderful family - my parents, brothers and sisters - on both sides of the water. Without them all would surely have been lost. My beautiful wife has loved me without regard to my quirkiness and foibles and, through many cold winters and delayed springs, has graced me with her unwavering love and the gift of three energetic and brilliant children who keep both of us alive and dancing into the future.

And dance we shall, into our blessed and joyful future, as
Children Of Light.

"GOD loves you – act like it!"

— Grace

VI

CONTENTS

PROLOGUE

An Impure Silence

An impure silence awakened him from an incomplete dream into a raging reality ... ...

Harsh wind whistled through his broken canopy. Super-heated metallic gases burnt his nostrils, creating a newly acquired feeling of panic that he'd never known before. With perfect intent, he pushed every wayward anxiety into the furthest reaches of his mind.

Slowly he grasped what evil had befallen him as he summoned the courage to reacquaint himself with exactly who he was – he was Lieutenant Kiyoshi Shou-ya! A pilot and officer in the advanced guard of Imperial Japan's Navy Air Service, although he looked like a mere boy from a distance; small, somewhat petite in stature. He'd become battle-hardened with a soul forged of Nipponese steel. Whatever he appeared to lack with his boyish sun-baked exterior he made up with a propensity for instantaneous violence. A broken eternity swam deep in his eyes. Veteran of many engagements across Greater Manchuria, he'd triumphed over his Emperor's foes in aerial combat with indoctrinated zeal. He was always victorious, ever ready to pounce. His staunchness was portrayed by his fierce countenance. With bursts of machinegun fire he'd vanquished his enemies without waver. With honed aerial combat skills he had created fireballs and debris fields far and wide. He exemplified pure malice for those daring to stand in the way of Imperial Japan's expansion across all of Southeast Asia, now even well beyond.

If they were unwilling to bend to the edicts of Japan's divine Emperor, they were unworthy of populating the earth.

During the morning's bold and daring attack he'd been stricken by ground fire. Obviously, in the chaos of battle, he'd been separated from his squadron. His tactical aerial samurai sword, his precious Zero fighter, had been fatally crippled! By what? He knew not. Yet, he was rapidly descending from an extremely high altitude, destination unknown, as all of his instruments were broken.

Scanning his immediate circumstance gave him little hope. His stricken craft was broken and shattered. Freezing winds burnt his face, neck and hands – he was in a dire struggle to survive. Only hard right rudder had any effect on direction. Yet, nothing he could do would have any effect on his disappearing attitude. Glancing through broken glass, he saw jagged exit wounds the length of his left wing's upper surfaces. Left aileron completely missing, hydraulic fluid streaming off the back edges of his once pristine aircraft. Rushing air sent violent shutters directly into the marrow of his bones. His prop stood stagnant and still like a tombstone awaiting an unwilling occupant.

If he could have seen his undercarriage, he'd have known he'd been hit by twin bursts of enemy anti-aircraft shells that exploded less than three feet off of his left wingtip. One took out the engine with the precision of a barbarian surgeon. The other impaled shrapnel into every system of his aircraft. Barely allowing his vertical stabilizer to stay adhered to the fuselage. His plane flew with the lost grace of a mortally wounded bird of prey.

With no aileron, his left flap frozen into an impossible position, all hydraulic fluid evaporated into the atmosphere of the frozen blue sky. Falling from the heights of a virtual blue wilderness; he could feel the tugging of the barren skies carrying him moment-by-moment ever further from his homeland. Lieutenant Kiyoshi yearned for the familiarity of home, a far off time and place known as Hiroshima.

Oh just one more chance to taste the delicacies of green tea ... ...

To hold his father's manuscripts on peaceful existence ... ...

To clutch his war books that expounded the glories of the battlefield ... ...

Lightheaded from blood loss, he could feel his life quickly falling away. Finally he managed to take stock of himself. As an imperial officer he'd been trained to ignore all pain and to push frailty firmly aside. But today that training was evaporating as quickly as his altitude. His left side had suffered a grievous wound. Unable to move his left fingers, with blood splattered all through the cockpit – his melted uniform confirmed his deepest fears. Whatever hit his craft had also penetrated and incinerated his mortal body!

For the first time in his warrior existence - an aerial combat ace two times over - he felt both naked and vulnerable. Somehow he'd allowed himself to be violently thrust into this newfound reality.

Seeing three massive peaks directly ahead, two were even glistening with snowcaps, he fought to glide his dead craft towards them. Their presence was his only hope of finding a landing that he might possibly survive. The Pacific Ocean was far too vast; without radio communication he'd never be found amongst its endless waves. As he fell below the third layer of clouds, pushing ever harder right pedal - his frayed rudder cable snapped! Immediately his broken fighter lunged towards a terminal finality.

Then, to seal his doom, his vertical stabilizer tore completely off!

Its catastrophic departure threw his once deadly fighter into an unrecoverable flat spin. Lieutenant Kiyoshi Shou-ya's feeling of impending doom amplified immensely. He knew that he wouldn't reach any of the hoped for promontories. Delirious with pain, death's certainty firmly grasped hold of his anxious spirit as broken protocols screamed within his soul.

His neurotransmitters functioned in gasps of primordial survival mode, keeping him alive long enough to glimpse a scene of pure perfection.

One brief flash of hope found him in his distress! It was a profound glimpse of heaven directly before him – *The Pure Land* - as he'd been taught. A target he'd sought his entire life; today it wondrously appeared as rolling green hills of vibrant joy, a solitary tree stood stalwart proclaiming strength of life while a glorious herd of horses galloped away from him, exemplifying astonishing freedoms.

His broken advanced tactical fighter charted its own destruction by crashing onto a foreign land. With divine mercy it miraculously embraced a softer impact on the backside of a downhill slope, sparing its lone occupant an immediate grave. As puffs of green grasses and dark soils gently settled, Lieutenant Kiyoshi Shou-ya's imperial orders of being a merciless warrior hell-bent on a mission-of-death for the Emperor of Japan, took an abrupt turn into an immediate future where his true mission awaited.

A mission that this very day became a stark reality.

A reality from which heroes must be born, a profound reality that began in the furthest recesses of the dawn of time. Instigated by mankind's banishment from the Garden of Eden.

Kiyoshi's spectacularly silent crash onto a tiny speck of land would be used as a catalyst for a divinely ordained series of epic events, held as a myriad of closely guarded secrets. Hidden as a treasure trove to assist in GOD's chosen few to rediscover their ancient heritage. For them to lead the ongoing battle against the rapidly increasing darkness engulfing the entire world.

Held in a sacred trust, deep secrets from ages past, yet, now to be delivered directly by HIS supernatural righteousness, as a gift of love for HIS wayward children. Lost children, yes. But, miraculously destined to become HIS chosen warriors. Known in every generation as, *Children of Light*.

They just didn't know that their epic journey had begun … …

1

Little Girl Lost

In The Year Of Our LORD

1946

March 31ˢᵗ

It was a Sunday ………

LAUPAHOEHOE POINT, DISTRICT OF SOUTH HILO, ISLAND OF HAWAII

She was so lost, frightened, and angry to the point of hate.

Her father was dead and she wished that the man whom had replaced him would just leave and never come back – he was wicked to her every day and was trying to be at night as well.

Her mother drank and smoked and lied every day to her.

Above all else, she was lonely and saw no escape.

For growing up in paradise – this existence was a special form of hell.

Trees and foliage of a thousand shades of green dripped off of the eight hundred foot cliffs. Waterfalls fell so far that their cascades turned back to rain, gathered at the base of the cliffs and poured into the vast Pacific Ocean that pounded upon black sand beaches that absorbed their foam and spray. *Aama crabs*, shiny wet black and hiding in the sand, emerged to scavenge as they would amidst the chaos and thunder.

She grew up here, in East Windward Hawaii, where people knew not the beauty they were immersed in, nor the perils that she fought both within and without, for she was in mortal danger from the evil, possessed and demented man who had the audacity to be known as her stepfather. His breath had fumes

4

of death laced into it and his eyes were dead – mostly, but at times sparked with a spectrum of rage and lust that knew no boundaries. He harvested opihi, a half-shell delicacy, along the rocks on the coast and traded them mostly for beer and rye whiskey – some he saved for barter at the cockfights in the local camps – but he could never pick a winner since he never could see one in any format, species of animal or type of human being.

And when he lost, as he always did, every time it was someone else's fault. For like all losers, he could never ever accept the long list and huge stack of bad decisions he had piled one atop another.

Those losses and that rage had been what had driven her to flee to the small gazebo on the jagged and raging shoreline. She ran to escape, and she ran to find peace for a glimmer of time. This small gazebo was bamboo and ohia wood, with a faded tin roof of peeling green paint and moss growing on the northern edges of everything. It sat at the edge of the most pristine tidal pool, white sand bottom, black lava rock fringed with wisps of electric green grass edging it all around. The grass needed a good mowing, but for now it looked so soft as to have been made in Heaven.

Today she came completely distraught. She had hidden her problems so well from the world until this very moment – but today something snapped deep within her. One fire had been extinguished and there was no stopping the cascade of tears, hate wrapped in fear and all encased in sorrow.

Where was her Daddy? And why had he abandoned her – death was no excuse!

And as she cried, time moved like trapped water, all as one brilliant beam of light broke through heavy clouds of grey that pushed against the cliffs above her. That single shaft of light walked slowly across the mountainside. Lingered on the tidal pool, and upon the gazebo with a lost little girl holding her knees and sobbing. Her hair was in a full-blown mess falling over her face to hide her shame from the beauty saturating all around her.

Tears flowed down her face, through her long long hair and pooled on the cement bench she sat upon.

Her shattered family consumed all of her dreams, and beauty would not console her.

But, what she did not see and what she had not noticed was the lone figure standing in the tidal pool in the white sand portion that was about three feet deep. Standing still, motionless and draped with a worn, patched and ready to be thrown net, the fisherman had his eyes upon a very tight ball of fish directly in front of him – but his attention was upon the frail girl huddled in the gazebo above. He threw his net perfectly; it spread out into a circle falling upon the school of fish that darted in, not out, and together they were trapped and doomed at the same time. He smiled calmly as he tightened the bottom line pulling the net into a ball with dozens of fishes for him, his families and his neighbors. Tonight they would all eat well – for fresh fish, a scoop of rice and freshly picked vegetables out of the garden would make for a wonderful evening.

Yet all of that meant virtually nothing. Of course, it was nice to provide for one's family, but as for now and as for this moment in time – it was the little girl lost sobbing in the gazebo that needed his full attention. So he tied off his catch, for dinner could wait, and climbed out of the water over the lava stones and stood on the rock before her.

Without saying a word, he gently lifted her face to see into his eyes and through the tears of pain and years of hurt, she locked onto his quiet and gentle gaze. He wiped one tear away, of the many, and said –

"Today I shall pray to GOD ALMIGHTY for you and your situation shall never ever be the same." And with a soft smile he asked her, "Are you ready?"

And with the exhaustion of the ages – she simply nodded yes.

So he prayed with tremendous power and authority in a voice so soft that only they could hear, "May the LORD bless you and keep you for HE shall shine HIS light upon you and keep you from this very moment forward. HE shall guide you in all that you endeavor and shall choose to do. Nothing that you wish shall be held back from you from this very moment forward. May wonder and amazement chase you down. May the kindness of strangers become so common for you that it is barely worth noticing – although you will always notice and be kind in return. May the LORD GOD ALMIGHTY give you peace, understanding and calm that transcends' the ages. You shall dip your feet in oil – the oil of gladness - and you shall enjoy prosperity unlike few others of your generation. You shall see angels and command them, as you deem fit and proper. You shall live a wondrous adventurous existence full of abundantly simple joys of being surprised by that, which occurs around you. And, above all else – may love saturate all that you do and may you know the personal and infinite closeness of GOD's love at an intimate level." Then he stopped, looked at her – had a very deep thought – then said, "And one more blessing shall be upon you – for you shall be embraced by a future of infinite possibilities!"

She was crying no more and looked somewhere between perplexed and shocked. Then he said, "Of course, just like me and many before us, you shall become a *Fisher of Men*. Now help me get this net out of the water – for we both have work to be done and wondrous lives to live! And my dear – both of those are here and now as we race into the burning fires of time known as the future."

He had her help him load the fish into an old pickup truck with a massive homemade cooler in the back. The cooler was packed to the brim, tails sticking out all of the way around the lid, which was squashed upon them. For her efforts – he gave her two fish, two very large fish – almost more that a young girl could carry. With that simple gesture, he said, "One last blessing for you, my fine and sweet young lady, may JESUS himself teach you and bless you, may HE forever hold you in HIS arms and may HE give you the gift of music in dance and song. You shall dance with kings of the Earth, laugh with their children and give counsel to their wives. You will never need to chase or pursue anyone or anything – for it and they shall come to you – in the name of power, wisdom and glory – JESUS! Amen."

Those simple words – 'my fine and sweet young lady' - she had never heard spoken before, ever, in her life. That rare kindness broke her composure once again – and she dropped her fish on the cement bench, laid her head on the picnic table and cried the final throws of a life that came to an abrupt end in exchange for a new life that would now define the person to whom she was to be.

Then, before he drove back the rugged trail of a road that switch-backed and worked it's way back up the *pali,* being a shear seacliff, to the highway far above – he said one final thing, "Remember, Grace, you are a gift from GOD, and that HE is the CREATOR OF THE UNIVERSE and of all things both in Heaven and on Earth. HE knows you by name, Grace Leilani Lee. HE knew you long before you were born and HE will watch, care and prosper you in all things – all the way through every trial and revelation, during every joy and happiness, even long after HE calls you home to be with HIM. Bless you, young Grace; hope to see you soon!"

A soft gentle rain fell like mist as clouds rolled and tumbled through the royal groves of koa cloud forests in the valleys above. Those soft wisps of broken slowly falling bits of grey pushed into the green – feeding life to the plants, the Earth and endless fields of vertical lush ferns that somehow clung to the volcanic crags above. All the while - one small girl in one lone gazebo on a slice of lava that jutted into the vast Pacific sat bathed in a single column of light with a most profound brilliant rainbow before her. She had just had her first encounter with an angel of GOD and was totally clueless that it had even happened.

All she knew was that she had never felt so light, the burdens of the world were gone – the scars burned deep into the soul of her eyes were healed, and of all new things – she felt truly, without any proof of any kind, saturated in love for the first time in her young world –and that, alone, was the miracle!

Dancing, singing new made up songs to an old familiar melody she climbed back up the trail to home. What she failed to see was that the old multi-colored beat-to-death pickup truck, with her newfound friend and mentor left no tire tracks! Along with the simple fact that the beam of light from Heaven above followed her and spotted her way long past sunset as she lazily walked homewards. Ginger, along with hosts of many other species of tropical flowers, bloomed along the way. A touch of the fragrance of another world lingered thick from the heavy air created by the fresh falling rain. It strangely had the fragrance of vanilla mixed with *pikake,* a sweetly potent white jasmine flower growing as an intertwined vine along the jungle trail. Although she could not place it, for it was a faded whisper of dreams yet to be pursued.

All of that mattered not - for she had two fishes for dinner! And, finally, all was right with her small world!

*   *   *   *   *   *   *

Although everything had changed deep within her spirit, virtually nothing had changed with her circumstance. Her mother lied and fretted in an endless loop of confusion. Her stepfather rarely showed his pockmarked face. He'd never come home the night before. It was best that way. Saved her mother from his savage foulmouthed attacks. Saved young Grace from his perverted advances.

They'd had the two fish her newfound friend, Gabriel, had gifted to her the evening prior. Bit of rice, some star fruit off of the valley tree tucked away behind their shanty, very best dinner she'd eaten in weeks, maybe even months.

Up before dawn, Grace had a plan. Today, yes this very day! She had hope invade her essence, and with that, she planned on changing her world. Hope was a new feeling for her. A spiritual awakening she'd never had before, it embraced her for the very first time in her entire lifetime. Today she planned on signing herself up for school!

Laupahoehoe School was less that a short mile's hike from the shack her parents had commandeered along the jagged coastline. She didn't know it, but they were squatters on a property abandoned by others. Too isolated by the Hamakua's nastiest terrain, it had been hastily built from pallet wood, straightened nails and rusty throwaway tin roofing panels.

Ugly and strangely positioned, tucked at the terminal edge of a valley's walls, it was too steep for any normal access trail. Only the ocean pathway at extreme low tide provided a means to move beyond the valley's limited confines; One and a half rooms with a jungle outhouse; a version of Hawaiian squalor, which created terrible conditions for a child to be trapped within. Solitude of a verdant jungle thick and lush gave it a semblance of serenity, yet it was merely a green veneer hiding the putrid interior, which had become brutal mean.

Grace picked her way along the ocean trail, first glimmers of sunlight pranced far along the eastern horizon. She'd become very adept at navigating mossy rocks and tight jungle pathways. She did it light-hearted, even with a sense of tremendous expectation, for today she was going to introduce herself to a teacher at the school. She cared not which one; for she was unsure of what grade she was even supposed to be in.

Grace hadn't attended school for at least three years, upon reflection, maybe four ... ...

Popping out of a sharp razor-thin footpath halfway up the pali, she came onto the broken road less than a quarter mile from the edge of the village. Not too far now, she positively beamed with anticipation!

Grace was obviously the first to arrive, she didn't mind as an overwhelming fragrance of pikake flowers scented the morning's dawn. Monday morning, early spring, sunlight now creating another effervescent Hawaiian day, shadows cast far across the school's freshly mowed lawn. Small waves burst against The Point's outer lava rock coastline - creating a suspended vapor of translucent salt mist. All as the dawn held it's breath for a new day to fully appear.

Slowly other students came and gathered, talking and jostling amongst themselves. A few looked Grace's way and smiled. She shyly smiled in acknowledgment. Happiness was, like hope, a brand new sensation. She greatly liked the feeling. She waved at them, they eagerly waved back although they knew her not.

Today she hoped to change that, for today she yearned to be included into their world of joy and newfound friendships. Just as she made that wave - it was as if the very atmosphere swallowed joy itself! From the extreme northeast a wicked pulse, a split second of liquid lightning flashed pure white as a foreboding of imminent doom entered everyone's world!

All the children gasped in unison, time ceased to function ... ...

First it was the rumblings of smaller rocks, then the crashing of boulders being sucked out from the shoreline. A startled flock of egrets leaped simultaneously into the golden dawn's light! Looking for altitude, the only safe direction to possibly survive.

Some of the children climbed for safety into the dense foliage of the mountainside's soft embrace. Others, far too curious, were lured towards the seabed and its newly exposed reef barrens. Fish flopping - some huge - were floundering in newly isolated pools. Seaweed - still glistening electric green - helped to soften rumblings of death from the rocks and boulders tumbling and rolling.

There was no pause, just all things building to a crescendo of doom.

Grace sprinted southwards. Looking for an escape from the massive whitewater, furious with hunger it ravaged vegetation off of the shear rock seacliff while climbing the vertical rock promontory. The pulse had an agenda of devastation. Such a dreadful reality; the tsunami resulted from a violent up thrust megaquake, casting itself outwards at great speed from the seafloor off the Aleutian Islands. It delivered its liquid wrath to here, at this very hour and at this very place, Laupahoehoe Peninsula. April 1st, 1946 and the wicked tsunami of liquid death arrived without wavering, notice or care of whom it consumed.

Grace found herself caught instantly within its deadly grasp. As the second, third and fourth waves scoured the once pristine shoreline she tumbled and rolled. She was battered and crushed. In between gasps, she got out a few bits and pieces of screams. Hoping for some help from those who would have been her classmates, her teachers … … her newfound friends. Grace's screams echoed off the seacliff walls unanswered. Her pleadings forlornly turned from shock and awe to gasps of begging. Then slowly, methodically the ocean swept her far away.

Somehow Grace clawed her way through the violent maelstrom. She saw a tiny glimmer of the faintest light shining in the upper reaches of her newfound pulverized reality. Grinding flotsam; splintered buildings, trees and foliage that used to be so alive - now all dying one together - being shredded by an ocean gone insane with rage. Only that singular burst of light permeated the darkness. One route to freedom! Grace, with all strength allotted, clawed towards that light with but one tiny whisper of breath remaining. Desperately injured and too battered to think - only react - she found the surface merely inches beyond her grasp.

Silently all things faded into the velvet embrace of the darkest night … …

* * * * * * *

THE REALM

Awaking, Grace found herself sitting in a classroom with others of her own age. Seemed like many were the exact same souls she'd waved and smiled at down at The Point, near the moss-covered gazebo, just moments prior. Grace couldn't help but notice how everything felt so strange. It was if she was captured within *The Living Now*, such a wonderful sensation.

Her desk was one of twenty-five newly formed into a half-circle, all facing the TEACHER whom was dressed in glowing pure white linen. Grace smiled, even laughed a bit at how light-hearted she had become. She had not a care. All things embraced a quiet perfection newly acquired.

10

Looking closely, she couldn't help but notice how the TEACHER shown brilliant ethereal pure. HE smiled while lifting HIS nail pierced hands to begin the day's lessons ... ...

2

The Point

IN THE YEAR OF OUR LORD,

1976

*EXACTLY THIRTY YEARS LATER...

LAUPAHOEHOE POINT, DISTRICT OF SOUTH HILO, ISLAND OF HAWAII

Thick dense moss of electric greens of many shades and hues still covered the northern portions of the gazebo – all northern portions. It had gotten a new roof of tin for the salt spray had finally destroyed the last one beyond repair. Some various attempts at graffiti had been obscured by some various attempts of painting by the maintenance guys trying to cover them up. Seemed like nothing could change the basic character of the small shelter that managed to stand through the storms of time.

The ocean still roared, the cliffs still stood motionless against the onslaught of clouds, mist and fog. Vegetation still dripped from them at impossible angles. The switchback road had been paved – poorly – and was still more or less gravel in spite of the attempted 'face lift'. Aqua blue tranquility still radiated from the tidal pool – which seemed to maintain an eerily calm presence in the huge foaming jets of shame that the ocean exploded upon the barrier of lava surrounding it.

Sun dried exoskeletons, bleached pale pink, clung to the rocks with eight forgotten legs. They dotted the black lava in perfect wholeness and at strange angles and locations. Many aama crabs shed their outer wear as needed to grow – as one generation displaced the next in the quest for food, shelter and the perpetual dance of life at the edge of the wild sea.

One other thing had changed down at The Point. Its leaf of lava, jutting northeastward into the Pacific Ocean, which stretched forever, had a new marker of hand cut stone, polished, sitting on the knoll nestled in pine overlooking the gazebo that had been placed inconspicuously. It was not majestic, for things made by man rarely are; it was simply there by need. The date, inscribed upon its face read April 1, 1946. Below that date was a list of twenty-four names etched upon it for all to see, although very few even noticed. Most in the community knew intuitively that there were names missing that should have been etched there as well, but with that day's chaos, broken communications and the adversary of time, who would ever know? There were those whom had placed flower *leis* that hung on it and lay near it. Half alive but mostly dead petals of different sun baked and rain washed flower arrangements lay beside it in disarray. That little monument to an epic *tsunami* [seismic wave] event decades before was new, as was the generation currently sitting in the gazebo. A small gathering of friends playing cards and drinking beer on a late Friday afternoon of perpetual summer.

Seven young men, *The Boys*, set there speechless – an extraordinary event in and of itself! They were watching a stunningly gorgeous lady in the tidal pool about fifty yards away. Her beauty, elegance and liquid motion had them, pure red-blooded American males, captivated and silent.

They all hid their cards either by holding them to their chests or by smashing them face down on the table before them. The conversation went counter clockwise in rapid fire around the table.

"Who is she?"

"How old is she?"

"What is she fishing for, there, in that shallow water?"

"I want a wife like that!"

"Isn't that your cousin?"

"I wish …………"

"Well, how old is she?"

"Dad always said she could have been Miss Hawaii 'back in the day'. He said she was, and always has been, beautiful."

"She could be Miss Hawaii now."

"Wait! You know this lady?"

"Well, who is she?"

Nalu [ocean wave], bringing his cards down from his chest and purposely putting them directly before him face down, said, "She is Grace Lee, my far distant *Auntie*. She is even more wonderful than she looks. She was never Miss Hawaii, although she had been encouraged to try out. She is so beautiful it hurts. I believe she teaches *hula* [ancient Polynesian dance] at the old folks home in Hilo now and then. If you remember, she was the Hula Babe in many of the TV commercials over the years. As good as she dances, you should hear her sing!"

"Wait a second, she's your Auntie?! Does she have daughters? What else have you been hiding from us besides those cards?" blurted out William [conqueror] across from Nalu with a startled expression – for he thought he knew Nalu – and this new factoid really got him.

"How old is she? I can't tell – you all must remember that I'm from Kansas, and we don't have women like that!" said Jesse [upright, GOD exists] with a simple statement of fact mixed with confused awe.

Nalu looked, smiled and said via deadpan delivery, "Early forties – at least."

"No way!"

Gasps .... then more gasps mixed with disbelief. And then, even more gasps of awe.

Everything got real quiet. Poker halted, everybody laid their cards down, letting it sink in – that beauty had no time limits and that age was relative to whom and how they wore it. Everyone had laid their cards face down, except for William, who noticed he'd screwed up and quickly flipped them over to hide his hand. He thought - at least no one noticed!

Samuel [heroic, observant, capable] noticed and immediately folded.

By undeclared need, and virtually in unison, they all got up to get a closer look at Nalu's Auntie. They softly walked on the short trail covered in ironwood pine needles over to the tidal pool where Grace was fishing and found her to be more tantalizing and beyond all expectations.

By this stage everyone's expectations were off the charts.

Grace was fishing and singing a new song she just created calling in her evenings' dinner. She had a simple bamboo pole, cut to about twelve feet in length with thirty-pound test line tied to the end. Using a small neon lure bought at the local *Mom-N-Pop* store up the road – she cast the line to the far side of the tidal pool, near the entrance to the sea beyond. She cast with poise and little effort, laying the line exactly where it needed to be.

All of the young men stood in awe - knowing how hard that cast, which she had just made look so effortless, really was.

Grace had used smashed anchovies mixed with old stale bread for bait – but then, by fluke she'd discovered these neon lures and greatly liked the fact that they didn't make her hands smell. But that was years ago, and today, she

14

simply sang, "… *oh Mr. Big Fish won't you come out today* … " She laughed at the lyrics knowing how foolish they sounded – but she put as much soft elegance into them as possible – certainly more than they deserved!

And then, as the tidal pool 'breathed' with a slight surge outward, a fairly large fish struck her lure. Grace then simply turned, saw she had admirers, smiled and walked up the gravel beach dragging her catch to shore. She had a twenty-five plus pound *ulua* on the line. It struggled. She beached it and walked back to inspect GOD's bounty.

By then all of the young men had crowded round. Not one of them had ever caught such an excellent specimen in such shallow waters and all of them considered themselves fishermen.

Grace walked through the crowd, knelt down and removed the hook, then did something that would become legend with this small group of admirers. She petted the ulua and spoke to it. "I am so sorry to have disturbed your swim today. Please accept my apologies and live a full life," and with a faint smile added, "and have many, many *keikis* [children]"

Then, carrying it back into the tidal pool, she left it go in about three feet of water and aiming it at the tiny channel outlet to the open ocean beyond.

Nalu, speaking for all of them, blurted out, "Auntie, how could you let him go?!"

Grace walked over to Nalu and embraced him.

Every guy there wished they were Nalu.

She said, "Oh but my favorite nephew! He was just a mere baby for his kind. You know that type of ulua can get to over one hundred pounds! Who am I to shorten his days of joy in that vast and bountiful ocean?" Then she smiled and laughed, "Besides, I was thinking more like *kumu* for dinner tonight."

She surveyed her nephew's 'tribe' and asked, "Nalu, I believe you have never introduced me to your wayward friends. Are these the young men you've been surfing with - amongst other things?"

Grace gave Nalu a knowing look that only an 'Auntie' could give. Then she smiled, looked at the motley crew of surfers and such and allowed her nephew to introduce his friends. All of them, except for Nalu, stood at attention with schoolboy looks scuffing their feet in the dirt and cinder shyly waiting to be called one by one. Every single one of them was in total awe and stunned by this gorgeous lady of elegance, charm and obvious brilliance standing before them.

Grace shown like an intense light of being before them, and they gazed down from their unworthiness.

Grace noticed their discomfort, so being worthy of her name, asked "Now which one is this?" offering her hand to the tall dark Japanese young man on the far left of the row.

"Auntie, this is Akina [honesty, strength] he's originally from Kaneohe over on Oahu. Much like you, he can fish – although he really can't sing them onto his line – in fact I don't think he can sing at all!" Grace gave Nalu a look that did not include appreciating his small attempt at humor. Grace looked at Akina, "One of these days you will sing gloriously, and it will shock you where."

Nalu continued down the line, "Auntie this gentleman, " having learned from a single glance, "This friend is Jonathan [strength of GOD]. We call him *Aina* [dirt, land, real estate, property]; he loves to grow things. His garden is always producing something. Today it's onions and lettuce. When he's having a really bad day, we call him 'Dirt'. Jonathan is from the backside of Wood Valley down in Kau."

Jonathan smiled and gave Grace a big hug, as all good local boys would, a flash of color jumped through her eyes flashing crystal green – he felt like he'd just been scanned by something sacred – and didn't know how to reconcile feeling both loved and unworthy simultaneously.

Nalu, not seeing all that had occurred and failing to grasp such things, continued with the introductions, "Auntie [family friend related or unrelated], this is 'Pancho' – he's our resident *Paniolo* [cowboy], but kindergarten was a little hard on him and so were his classmates. He loves horses like his whole family does – they live on the backside of Waimea raising cattle. Their horses are the happiest horses on Earth; they roll in green pasture, prance in Heaven and lounge in the Pacific mists. I think only your Arabians have it better, Auntie."

Grace, in a moment of instant recognition, "So your family has the paints and raises the shiny charolais beef above Hawi Town – that would be *Haiwiki Ranch* [Heavenly Ranch]!"

"My real name is Samuel Kealoha; they just call me 'Pancho' because my long distant uncle was Mexican Panilolo and one of the original cattle wranglers brought in for the King's herds. So Auntie Grace, you have the ranch up *Mauna Kea* with the only herd of Arabians in the state – talk about happy horses! They have everything they could ever want, and the most beautiful rider to make them even look better." Then in his own epiphany of recognition, "You are the one that rides with the *Daughters of Hawaii* [descendants of royalty] in the parade on *King Kam Day* [celebration for revered King Kamehameha]!"

They looked at each other and smiled, their paths would cross again. The horse community and associated round ups was a small fellowship of souls on the Big Island.

16

"OK, horse lovers, Auntie, this is Makani [windy] – we call him 'Windy' he loves to sail," Nalu said. What he left out of the introduction wasn't just that Makani sailed and was an excellent wind surfer – a sport just becoming popular, especially on Maui - but that Windy loved to talk all of the time and without restraint. Yet, they all loved him anyways. Through the years, they had all learned to just cut him off in mid-sentence as needed, especially if girls were involved.

Grace gave Makani a smile that just exploded upon him, and with great conviction, leveled him and bonded with him by saying, " I've been involved in two circumnavigations. We took the southern route both times; sailing, even the mere thought of it, takes me back to the early years of my adventures – and those were the most wonderful times!" Then she added, "So you sail?"

"I do, Auntie, but on such a micro scale compared to that. What I've always dreamt of. I windsurf – we've found a place on Maui near Paia Town that's just awesome for it. I think we need better equipment – it seems everything breaks at Hookipa." Then looking down, he added, "Thank GOD that it has been only equipment – and not me." Then, living up to his name, he added, "Now if I were Nalu the shore pound wouldn't scare me so much after losing the sail and tearing the board to shreds on the left point."

He went to say more, but was politely cut off by Grace, "Oh Makani – even you should know that staying near the right point would save you much anxiety and equipment failure."

Every guy there looked at each other and thought exactly the same thing – how does she even know that?

Nalu pondered the Hookipa comment, then said, "Auntie, this is William Ishi, our resident big wave rider. William has the little boat we all try to fill up with *ono*, *ahi*, *mahi* and an occasional *marlin*. He takes us out of Pohoiki Bay. Seems we usually catch ono off that coast - especially to the south, *Kalapana Beach* way. And Auntie, William sang in the rock-n-roll group *The Misfits*."

William smiled at Grace. Grace gave him the look that women have given men for ten thousand years – it simply stated: Not now! Not ever! Then she softened a little bit and asked," So William, do you use live bait or lures when you fish along that majestic shoreline?"

William was a little startled by that choice of subject – especially after 'the look', but he, ever being quick to respond, "Usually lures, but we put some *ika* [squid] tentacles stringing within the skirts to help them make up their minds to strike."

Grace was somewhat impressed, having never heard of that method before in all of her years. She said "Nice, I can see how that would help – sometimes fish need a little something extra to commit, much like all of us."

She shook Williams hand, even though he obviously would have preferred a hug.

Grace was trying her best to not feel like she'd been groped.

"Alright, now who is this one?" She'd finally gotten to the only blonde in the group, medium built with wavy hair and a tan that highlighted a smile that shown to Heaven on the darkest night.

"I'm Jesse Fairman – these friends call me *Haole* [caucasian] - I certainly prefer Jesse," he reached out his hand for a proper handshake, after seeing William's results and instead got the warmest hug and a wonderful kiss on both cheeks.

Jesse laughed, Grace held him by both shoulders and smiled, William was stunned. The others all marveled at her response to their friend from Kansas.

Nalu blurted out, "What is it with you?! Does every girl on Earth just naturally love you?! Unbelievable!"

Grace could care less, she looked at him and asked, "What is it that you love, Jesse Fairman?"

"Girls like you Auntie." He quietly answered, there was no lying of any kind, ever, in Jesse.

Grace actually laughed like a schoolgirl for a few seconds. Yet she never lost her composure and softly said, "You must forever be careful whom you entrust your heart to. They must be kind, considerate, loving above all else, light hearted, full of song and dance and laughter. And, I hope not necessary, but easy to forgive." And then she gave him that piercing look of love with so deep of a meaning – and then, hugged him again! The first hug was for friendly acknowledgement. The second hug was for her – after all, she was a woman!

Every guy there just stared at Jesse and shook their heads.

Jesse said, a little too embarrassed, "What – so ladies love me?" as he looked at his somewhat 'miffed' buddies.

And William, just slowly shaking his head thought, hey – I didn't even get one hug – just a handshake – and that confounded him to no end.

Introductions completed, awkwardly at best, Grace broke the strangeness that engulfed them with a light-hearted question, "So Nalu, is that your guitar?"

pointing at a hand-me-down case, frayed, scuffed and with rusty hinges leaning in the corner of the gazebo.

"Yea Auntie, *Uncle* [family friend related or unrelated] gave it to me a few years back – I think he hoped I'd get some skills like others in the family," not too subtly looking at her with eye brows raised, "Maybe now would be an excellent time for a *sukoshi* [small, tiny] lesson ... "

He walked over, unfastened two snaps and pried open the third. Getting it unsnapped, he lifted the old Martin, worn and with ends of guitar strings kinked and pointing in impossible angles, out of the case and presented it to Grace.

"Oh Auntie, can you sing for us wayward and lost souls, here in this place of beauty. For only a song from you could improve such a place as this." He didn't even know where those words had come from and they startled him as much as anyone – all of his friends looked at Nalu as if they had never known him.

Grace intuitively adjusted her playing for both the worn strings and the slightly warped neck. She gently sang a new song for her, one she'd just heard a few days prior. The song was *If* by *Bread*, and she sang it with such quiet conviction, with her own rendition and emphasis – and then after an improvised guitar solo – she sang it in Hawaiian to the young men, whom now had melted into little boys, mesmerized by the divine being performing before them.

Time stopped, a song went out and the spark of life lit up a small sliver of lava on a far away coastline in the middle of an endless ocean, on a speck of blue, in a universe that had obviously been created by a magnificent GOD.

A single shaft of light, that nobody noticed, broke through the ominous late afternoon clouds that were crushed against the cliffs behind them and lit the gazebo and the tidal pool as it danced about.

Not a one of them noticed, and not a one of them cared.

Nalu laid his head down and cried – the Hawaiian version had crushed him deep inside. It was too close to the heart for words.

None of the other young men noticed – they all just sat stunned by the performance they had just witnessed – except for William, who also enjoyed the song – but was still stewing on the fact he'd gotten a handshake and not the hug. William also was incapable of processing the fact that ladies like Grace really existed. He'd always been with 'clueless' or 'high mileage' varieties in his life, and Grace was a 'fact' he just couldn't come to grips with or even begin to fathom.

Then, as if hit by a small jolt of electric, they all stood and applauded.

Grace blushed, smiled and sat the guitar down in the mossy corner to the north. "I've better go get dinner – my fish is ready to volunteer."

Nalu blurted out, "You just can't leave us like this Auntie! Don't you have something more for us?"

The SPIRIT OF THE SOVEREIGN LORD stirred within her, and she knew that this was the real reason she'd been put here today, with her nephew's crew and at this very point in time, so she asked, "Would you mind if I prayed for all of you?"

Grace smiled and thought; now they are finally ready – thank you, FATHER. The impossible beam of light that had broken through from above intensified to the point where the moisture in the ground started to evaporate into wispy gasps of fog, drifting towards Heaven in tiny rivulets of joy at a pace so slow as to appear to be suspended in time and space.

Then with perfect timing, and in a voice so gentle and kind, Grace asked, once more, very directly and with tremendous simplicity, "Would you mind if I pray to GOD ALMIGHTY for you fine young men?"

They had already nodded, although William and Jesse were a little unsettled by the question at some primal level they couldn't put a finger on – but even they, the heathens, bowed their heads in the presence of the divine – so Grace began.

"Oh FATHER, LORD OF THE UNIVERSE, CREATOR of all things – both in Heaven and on Earth, we praise YOU for YOUR goodness, YOUR love and YOUR kindnesses. Thank you LORD! Today is the day! Now is the time! Please watch over these young men all of the days of their lives. Keep them clean, healthy – full of wisdom beyond their years. I thank YOU for putting them before me today – what a joy to behold! Please FATHER, give them love in such abundance that it overflows on all around them. Teach them that it's the little moments in time that really matter in the tapestry of life that YOU, FATHER, weave together to give their lives meaning and joy. Give them the dreams of their youth and tremendous bounty as resource to further YOUR kingdom and their lives. Shall you call on them to be heroes, may they instantly accept that divine invitation without hesitation or thought – and may they succeed at every task great or small, finite or unending that YOU place before them. YOU shall dip their feet in oil and place tremendous riches in their hearts and in their hands. May they know YOUR heart on such a level that they overflow in beauty and greatness so as to be infectious to all around them. May they even be a blessing when they are grumpy, tired and weary of life's lessons. Fill their lives with YOUR blessings of prosperity, the gift of travel to places as yet unknown and to the furthest reaches of this gift called Earth. May they be ambassadors for YOU to wherever YOU choose to send them. Give them adventure, fun, excitement, innovation, skills, open doors and a hedge of protection that can't be breached even by the Armies Of Darkness. May YOU, KING OF THE ANGEL ARMIES, march with them into battles as yet unknown and protect them by YOUR ALMIGHTY outstretched arm. Please, FATHER, give them the absolute simple joy of being surprised."

Then Grace took two steps forward and with great kindness and conviction said, "The LORD shall bless you and keep you. HE shall shine HIS light upon you. HE shall gift you with all the abundance of this beautiful land, hold you in HIS arms all of the days of your life, and personally welcome you at the gates of Heaven with the words: 'Well done my good and faithful servant!'"

Time itself froze, the air stood still, no sound could be heard even though waves crashed upon the shore just a stone's throw away – and a small group of foolish young men had been touched by the holy with a single heartfelt prayer given by Grace to the one true LIVING GOD – and those same, now changed, young men would never be the same.

Never, ever, ever be the same.

It is amazing what one prayer can do in this world of confusion and rapid paced lives for those who don't even know how desperately they need it, and sadly, don't even know to ask.

Then Grace passed on one of the most wonderful secrets of the universe to them, "GOD spoke everything that is, and was, and ever will be into existence by declaring it with the sound of HIS voice. As *Children of Light* [Christians], we are heirs to that authority – and that primal vibration still resonates - so whatever you speak into being shall occur, and whatever you curse into oblivion shall soon crumble and be crushed by the forces of GOD's mighty power. Never to ruin you, or yours, again. So always speak life into all around you, especially to those whom you love."

As if on cue, and with a mighty force, the relentless pressure of over 2,400 miles of trade winds pushed low hanging bundles of clouds against the immovable wall of green rocky seacliffs - crushing the clouds into a great volume of rain – now dumping as sheets upon the gathering of souls in the tiny gazebo below.

Rain immersed the atmosphere with the smell of the ocean suspended in wave after wave of heavy downpours. They cascaded off the mountains and within seconds the myriad of tiny waterfalls within the fern gullies created a 'veil of tears' that tried to replenish the ocean with their crying, but the ocean was already full and could care less about the rain's anguish and sorrows.

The downpour was relentless and took over any chance of conversation as the noise level beating upon the tiny tin roof became completely overpowering.

And then it was gone. The one massive cloud had been vanquished against the vertical rock faces above as a strange but welcomed calm filled the still misty air, and Grace smiled at the young boys (to her) men (to them), grabbed her pole and lightly walked back to her 'hot spot' where she proceeded to make the faintest of motion to flick her lure into the tiny channel that fed into the ocean which raged against the slivers of rocks that splintered the horizon.

What a horizon it was! It went from crystal light green at the edge of the tidal pool to a thousand shades of green, blue, darkgrey as it distanced itself to the far point blending into the next wave of rain melting the sky at a distance impossible to gauge.

Her cast barely landed and dinner struck it just as the tidal pool 'breathed out', right on cue – a king kumu struck violently– flaming red orange, about twenty two inches and seven and a half pounds that hit like lightning! It didn't wish to be dinner, but dinner nonetheless it would become, after a brief and valiant struggle.

Once again the 'fishermen' watching this catch unfold could not have been more amazed if *Godzilla* had marched across The Point and asked directions to Waikiki. Mouths fell and eyes stared as she calmly and gently 'thanked' the kumu for his generosity then placed him on the ice in the cooler in the back of her brand new sparkling white Toyota Landcruiser.

Grace, noticing the rapt attention of the audience, walked back over to them and asked, "OK, exactly why are you here?" Once again employing the 'Auntie look' - which cuts through all fluff and crap – going to the deepest point where only the truth resides.

Nalu answered, "Auntie, these are my friends from St. Joe and Hilo High – except for William and Jesse whom are first year U.H.H. We try to get together once a month for *Maui Hold-Em*, which is some odd Texas poker game with our local Maui twist. Last month's winner has to provide some of his ill-gotten gains to provide an activity and a location for the following month's game. I won last month" – everyone sighed and grunted – "so my chosen activity was diving The Point – and now we're just starting the game, so I'm trying to take their easy money one more time!

"So, who's winning? And why the empty seat?" asked Grace – beyond observant.

Nalu continued, seemed he was the only one that could get past the 'stunned by her beauty thing', and said, "The empty seat is for Timmy. He went opihi picking last fall; no one has seen him since. The official report was body lost at sea and never recovered – search discontinued. He was the best waterman of us all, knew him since kindergarten days. We all really miss Timmy. He'd be here right now if he could, so we make a place for him - just in case."

Nalu sighed, then continued, "But on a lighter note, our activity today got us a cooler full of lobster for dinner – except for William's – they're more prawn sized!" Nalu added, "We have a few for you Auntie, maybe you could have lobster stuffed kumu for dinner?"

William just shook his head, "Prawns!"

Grace still having their full attention stood before them and with total conviction said, "Remember the prayer earlier – for from this day on; none of you will ever be the same! I must go now, but before I do FATHER says it is important that I speak life into each of you – so with the fondest love and *aloha* [love, hello, goodbye] from myself, but more importantly from HIM …….." She walked over and knelt beside William, "You shall live a life of extreme adventure, find love and fortune – your children will be awesome. You will be split between two worlds that shall rarely meet. Fortune will track you down and the kindness' that you perform will only occasionally be known, but shall be stored, eternally for you in Heaven." Then she stood and gave him a long hug, which he sorely needed.

Grace took a small motion to the left, found Akina, held his hand and said, "All of these islands shall be yours - except this one. The city calls, do not get lost in its inferior lights for oh too long. Seek the Light that never dims, forsakes or denies what is pure and holy. Hold on until love tracks you down – then never let go! Wealth shall be easy, but don't let that take away from those whom need you to notice their plight or noble objectives. The sooner you find CHRIST, the younger you will remain."

Grace got off her knees, took two steps and found Jonathan's bowed head with her left hand holding her right hand to the ever increasing glow above, she bluntly said, "You shall be the one all others ask for advice and guidance. Give it clearly, and remember where Love, Courage, Light and Wisdom come from – for with you, a calm shall overcome all stormy seas."

She slowly looked at Jonathan's bowed head wiped a tear from her eye – and then moved to Samuel, "Young Samuel – a leader amongst men you will become before your time. An awareness that is beyond most humans' senses shall cause you, at times, to see more than you wish. I pray that GOD ALMIGHTY gifts you with HIS grace abounding so that you are not overwhelmed by HIS special gift. You will be a hero, renowned across Hawaii *Nei* [fondness, reverence], and even the world. The world will not only know your name – but you shall be spoken of for generations and well into the far and distant future."

Then Grace found Makani, who stood in the mist, just outside of the gazebo's shelter, with a longing in his eyes touched with fear, she said, "Oh my wind blown friend – the wind will carry you far and you will be on more than one *Voyage Of Discovery*. You shall call Maui *"No Ka Oi"* [the very best], your home for a season. There you will find love, both of the girl of your dreams and of the ocean full of adventure. Be careful with both! GOD will know your whereabouts no matter how far you sail – give HIM praise and HE will give you glory!"

A small burst of wind blew just as she finished her blessing, and Makani went to speak but Grace touched his lips with two fingers to gently shush him – then wiped the tears from his eyes and walked back to find one of the two remaining.

Nalu stepped forward, but she walked past him to Jesse and actually gasped with joy, then as if radiating a light from within spoke, "You are overwhelmingly pursued by girls and lovers whom want you desperately for their own selfish gain - many wish to control you or possess your very soul. Flee from them all! Love is way different and truly pure in and of itself – seek love above all else and then, and only then, will your life be upon calm waters. You will and shall know love –when it finds you never let go. It is the only lifeline in the storms ahead. Not only will it save your life – but it will cleanse your soul. FATHER also says, "You can date anyone you want – but for you, my son, - it's important to marry Japanese."' Grace was stunned and more than perplexed by what had just burst out of her, but then finished with, "I see GOD's humor and directions are both still intact! Chase true love my dear blonde from Kansas!"

Nalu was the only one remaining, he felt somewhat left behind by all that had transpired, the fleeting thought had even crossed his mind – is there a blessing for me? Even one small blessing for me, Auntie?

Grace took a few deep breaths, sighed and slowly took three steps back to her fondest and favorite nephew – staring into his world of deep emotions. She laughed with kindness of the ages softly grasped both his cheeks into her hands and spoke with great authority – and announced to all around her, "You, Nalu, will be great in these islands, revered by many and lifted up as an example of both aloha and strength. You shall lead well into the future and shall be seated in the halls of power way ahead of your years. By popular demand you shall be elected to the highest levels in government and shall see past the petty spoils lesser men crave. Stay true to your core values, and all the state shall be given unto you until the very day that you choose to train the next generation. There is a green eyed girl out there, when she comes into your sights, do not miss her! She will be your love and companion all the days of your life and she will make you look good wherever you are! Oh my beloved nephew – you are always welcome all across Hawaii - for food and drink and song and dance, enjoy that aspect of aloha, for it is your duty to bring all of those to the floors and halls of power. Crush the very foundations of the political machine, so as to build up the people, as you continue the endless struggle with 'bamboo politics' and 'spoiled fruit cronyism'!"

Then, dancing in the mist on emerald green grass, Grace Leilani Lee got into her Toyota Land Cruiser with her kumu and lobsters for dinner, smiled, waved the *shaka*, and blasted up the pali.

She was gone in seconds after causing such a stirringly profound event in the lives of seven young men. They honestly did not have a clue of all that had transpired; they simply knew on some spiritual level that the divine had invaded their compact worlds, and that something had shattered both within them and the world that they were being propelled towards –their futures had just begun anew – as the ramifications of Grace's prayers were being cast in Heaven above.

It was the Year Of Our LORD, nineteen hundred seventy-six, on a tiny sliver of lava with wild waves crashing and a heavy rain, once again, getting ready to fall upon seven fishermen who would experience the very hand of GOD in such a way that could not be explained, only experienced, as the 'chosen' had through eons of time.

Then the clouds burst, their cards got scattered, and the game was called due to weather and a total lack of interest. Each of the seven resided in their own worlds as they piled into cars and trucks to head home to various points on the compass dial for the remainder of the weekend. Only Nalu stayed behind to gather the beer cans, *bento* [Japanese lunch box] lunch remnants, flown all over deck of cards – and try to grasp a glimpse of sanity while trashing the other items into the garbage can marked County of Hawaii beside the tiny haven with the moss on all northern exposures.

Nalu stared at the marching chain of squalls headed his way, layered far into the horizon that melted into the ocean with no discernable barrier between them. He looked without seeing and felt without knowing what had just happened. His confusion was warped by this overwhelming sense of relief and simple touch of joy it was contained in. His heart raced with a new type of excitement like he had never known. Grabbing his guitar, he sat down to play, got a far distant look in his eyes and plucked at the beginning notes of *If* with a faint sound of the rain keeping time to his musings – yet not to him - but to a drumbeat from far above.

Lingering scents of vanilla wafted in the air with tinges of his favorite lei flower intertwined – it was pikake vanilla mixed to make a new scent that was a prelude to the Heavenly Realm.

*   *   *   *   *   *   *

Pitch-black darkness was laced with fog off of the ocean as Nalu drove up the pali to the belt highway and into Hilo Town. Once home he found his mother and gave her the biggest hug from the deepest part of him, the biggest hug he'd given her since he was a little boy so many years prior.

That hug so overwhelmed his mother that she sat at the dinner table and cried.

Then Nalu walked over to his father, who was always so distant, and as he looked him squarely in the eyes and said, "Please forgive me Father, for rarely ever listening to you, ditching you time after time for others. I wish to tell you that I love you, respect you and from this moment on – I hope to do better as your son."

His father, a very stoic and proper blue-collar guy, for the first time in his adult life, was totally utterly speechless, overwhelmed with emotion, and he simply nodded his love and gave a faint smile of wise knowledge. Then he added, "Son, you honestly make me proud to be your dad; I love you too."

By those two simple acts of love, without measure, years of animosity had been crushed upon the ice of indifference – both shattered upon impact - and a family had been restored.

Nalu lay down to sleep pondering all that had occurred – so much of it made no sense and seemed so surreal as to wonder if it was actually possible to have happened in a single day. It is amazing what a day shall bring – and when intermingled with the divine – how wonderful a simple life in a normal world can become.

Then, being an eighteen-year-old boy, he asked one of his final questions of the day - deeply to himself – where is my green-eyed girl?

When his parents were finally alone, his father asked his mother a different question, "Do you think Nalu is alright, Mother?"

Nalu was more than 'alright'. He was six foot, two inches tall; it appeared that he had been chiseled out of light chocolate bronze and was a young Polynesian version of superman. His mother was Hawaiian–Chinese-Filipino, his father was Scotch-Irish-Portuguese-Hawaiian. His father worked at the docks for the longshoreman's union and coordinated shuffling containers both going to and coming from all points of the world. His mother was a librarian at the local college – U.H.H., the University of Hawaii at Hilo – or Uhhhhhhh ...... as some of the haole mainlanders loved to call it, very affectionately. They had one son,

Nalu. They had wished to have more but, alas, such was the reality in which they lived.

Nalu was their pride and joy. He came from an extremely long line of royalty on the Hawaiian side; his great-great-great-great grandmother had been *Alii* [royalty] and a favorite cousin of the great *King Kamehameha*. They could trace their lineage way back, beyond first contact. Nalu excelled in sports; he was a natural at both soccer and basketball, but even better at both guitar and occasionally dancing *haka* with the other young local men for a touch of Hawaiian at the various *luaus* and festivals.

But what Nalu really loved was surfing – and that is what his parents lost him to when he was about ten years old. Nalu surfed like the wind and frequented Honolii with the others, especially on larger days. By the time he was sixteen he was routinely surfing monster waves at not only Honolii, but at the lesser known and way more deadly breaks along the awesome northeast coast – Brewer's, Hakalau, Kolekole and even Tombstones. This fact he never discussed with his mom and dad; he hated to give them actual facts to worry about – they already worried way too much.

Especially about his associations.

It was his senior year at St. Joseph High School. The girls loved him, but he barely noticed. After going to school with them for twelve years – the nice ones he simply treated as sisters he never had, the not so nice ones he simply ignored.

A few days earlier, as he worked and entertained, while bussing tables at *Auntie Hula's Polynesian Revue and Hotel.* He was asked by a five-Mai-Tai's-into-the-wind, bleached stone-white and wearing nasty matching aloha shirts tourist couple, "What are you?"

In impeccable English, he said, "Please clarify your question, or is that more of a statement?"

The more than semi-drunk husband blurted out, "What are you, an American or what?"

Nalu looked at them and deadpanned, "I am an American – for that is my nationality. I am beyond proud to be a true American! But if you are asking what ethnic backgrounds reside within me – then the answer to that is - I am Hawaiian, Chinese, Filipino, Scotch, Irish, Portuguese, and there are whispers that I may have a touch of Russian, but none will claim it!"

And with that admonishment laced with facts, he moved on to the next batch of tables to bus, leaving a wide eyed tourist wife, who had instantly fallen in love with him and her stupefied husband who remained speechless.

Such conversations were the best part of his job, working for minimum wage and meager tips from cheap drunk tourists at Auntie Hula's, not so much.

Nalu was a walking representative of the United Nations via ethnic background. He was a super healthy and world-class athlete by raw exposure and training. He was a bronze child of GOD by divine breath – and above everything else – he was a typical Hawaiian in all that mattered.

And that night, after the 'Grace Encounter', Nalu the surfer, son, waiter, student, blessed, heathen, fisherman, sailor, lover, poet warrior and eventual servant of the MOST HIGH GOD – simply slept like an angel and dreamed vibrant dreams in *Technicolor* tones of joy like he never had before.

How a simple normal day with friends had turned into the extraordinary, was duly noted, filed under 'needs to be pondered' and put away with the laying of a head on a pillow and the shutting of the eyes. Then, going to a place of dreams of another world, a world that rarely intersects with the land of the living - where we, rush immersed into the reality of life – everyday, after day, after day.

3

Puff

Sheets of pounding rain racked the old Plymouth Valiant so hard it actually rocked slightly from the force of impact. It was a typical Hilo morning, crack of dawn – barely even the whisper of light far off in the in eastern horizon. Just enough illumination to backlight the rain marching with the trade winds, a massive host of clouds layered far off to the horizon and beyond.

It was going to rain all day and then some. Typical Hilo – anywhere else would flood into oblivion - but Hilo simply absorbed it and got lush in doing so.

Nalu, Akina, and Jesse sat stuffed into the hammered Valiant with three surfboards – the smell of wax, old – too many times used – stinky towels and not so up to date hygiene. It was 6:40 a.m. and not a one of them had showered for dawn patrol surf session at Honolii.

As the minutes ticked by, the dawn pushed a little bit of light onto the scene below. Nalu broke the quiet, "There! Told you, look at that set coming in!"

Akina deadpanned, "*Puff* is here."

Ever since they were children playing in the inside keiki waves, they had always equated Honolii with the song *Puff The Magic Dragon*, and the rarely seen, but always awesome, spitting tube waves that broke at the left point. When they 'spit' the compressed air from the collapsing tubes, *The Boys* likened it to Puff's fire breathing breath – after all, Puff was from Honolii – and this appeared to be evidence of his being present and accounted for.

Jesse gasped as he realized the actual scope and size of the sets being delivered from the northeast to Honolii Point's reef at the base of the sea cliff. There were six to eight waves per set with massive girth and wicked force. As the dawn backlit them and their fronts came into form, it was obvious that this was a true north swell that made Honolii surfing the stuff of legends.

Jesse, with fear in his voice, said, "Looks like it's twenty-five feet!" He took a breath, then added, "Or more!"

Nalu looked at Akina, knowing it was 'only ' six to eight, being true Hawaiian by underestimating every wave ever seen and known to man, said, "Nah, no way … maybe four."

Akina looking at Jesse, nodded his head and laughed, "Maybe three to four – but solid."

All Hawaiian wave measurements are taken on the backside, not the pathetic 'California' method of measuring the face. This allowed for an open ocean swell measurement – and allowed for a very subjective 'guesstimate' when it came to breaking waves. In this particular example, at this particular point break and with very peculiar local boy surfers and their white boy naïve friend, they were calling eighteen-foot faces, 'three to four'. This kept wimps from paddling out with them and their legends, as Hawaiian surfers, fully intact.

Then the clean up set swept through. Jesse gasped seeing the twenty-two foot barrels exploding. Trying to remain calm, Nalu said, "Well, now, that's probably a true five feet!"

Akina just opened the door, stepped into the falling rain and grabbed his board - well technically, it was his uncles' - an old pin-tailed dark blue stick with the golden-yellow *Lightning Bolt* logo on it. It probably had fifteen ding patches in a myriad of off colors, but it was a numbered and signed Jerry Lopez original. He had personally shaped it. For its function – it was of perfect form.

Akina, instantly soaked to the bone, grabbed the end of his leash while tucking the board under his arm and went trotting towards the trailhead – not waiting for anyone in the cold downburst. As the rain washed the morning stench off of him, it preened his senses to the fact he was alive and on his way out to surf with his old buddy Puff. Never even glancing back, he focused on getting to the beach below and not wiping out on the mossy covered rocks.

Nalu and Jesse were right behind him. Nalu had a new *Orchid Land Surfboards* pintail, shaped by his buddy Stan, off of Kilauea Avenue right in Hilo.

Stan was Hilo's best local shaper by a wide margin. Nalu had Stan put an extra layer of glass on the bottom. All of the Big Island surfbreaks suffered from way too many rocks – and lava rocks were as unforgiving as it got.

Jesse had a twenty-dollar special, waterlogged old brown piece of junk, yet he seemed to do rather well with it. Jesse, originally being from Kansas and being only two years into an extreme sport that ate people for breakfast without remorse or explanation.

Nalu looked at Jesse, and with a seriously blunt delivery, yelled at him over the roar of the wind, waves and rain, "Stay in the channel! From there, pick your waves carefully! And if you go – GO! Do not hesitate and make sure you at least make the drop! " Then laughing wildly, " … And don't screw up – what would I tell your mother?!"

Together the three sprinted into the raging Honolii stream, used its running current to push through the inside breakers, braved the chocolate waters filled with light debris and bugasse from the sugar field operations above, and, by skilled maneuvering, found themselves past the dirty inside freshwater zone and into the relatively pristine waters beyond. Open ocean salt water was so much warmer – upon hitting it their bodies relaxed somewhat and soaked up the only warmth available. Rain continued drenching them from above - but it was impossible to get any more wet.

Nalu paddled straight away into the last wave of the set, catching a right from mid-channels, showing off a little as they worked their way to the point.

Puff was going crazy with multiple standing tubes forcing their way upon the shelf and exploding against the undercut cliff face that was right there. Foam and violence filled the impact zone on the reef that formed the basis of the break and allowed it to work, upon occasion, so perfectly.

Unlike most days, where the sun baked you alive and thirst was ever present even when surrounded by boundless water, this morning with the curtains of rain whisking through – that was not an issue. Akina laid his head back and took a mighty drink during one exceptional downburst from a squall line - calm as could be - just radiating in the experience.

Jesse was wound so tight he was putting pressure dings in the edges of his board. As he realized he'd never been in surf like this before he thought, way too big! Way too big! Way too big! Like a cassette loop running through his brain.

Nalu and Akina paddled, without hesitation, into the next set of thunder coming through. Nalu caught the fourth wave, Akina the fifth. Both put on displays of applied skill – not caring for any kind of audience, just absolutely loving the moment of being alone with this wonderous form of bounty sent across the largest body of water on the planet.

Jesse watched from the relative safety of the channel trying to get up the courage to even attempt what his friends so competently displayed.

Hanolii's resident mystical creature roared, the seacliffs stood stalwart, *The Boys* played and Puff the Magic Dragon gave a performance to his chosen friends of the day, that few rarely saw – let alone participated in. Another day on the edge of Hilo Town came to life as daylight dawned and shook the godly and the heathen out of their slumbers. Sugar cane trucks started their dance on the mountain above. Technocrats contemplated getting to the county office building. Students looked at the rain and sighed. Parents looked at the rain and told their children to stay out of it. College professors thought it was a good day to take roll call and give a quiz. A *Young Brothers Ltd.* container barge rounded the end of the breakwater bringing that day's goods to port to get off-loaded in short order. The crop duster fleet remained grounded until further notice, water ran in the streets – Nalu looked at his wristwatch and thought – one more wave, hope the Valiant starts!

4

Shaka Wisdom

Senior year was fast coming to an end for this crop of St. Joseph High students. It was an excellent batch – a classic close-knit group of overachievers. Even the slackers were somewhat well behaved, at least while in school. The soccer team did fairly well, dominated the Big Island league – but got completely crushed when sent to Oahu for states. Most of them had much bigger dreams than winning a high school sports trophy. Although, one more for the glass case with "Class of '76" on it would have been bragging rights for decades to come. Didn't happen – they got over it and moved towards graduation.

Time went into a strange mode as graduation loomed – events, even small snippets, took on an unearthly quality – poignancies tinged with sadness. The last chemistry class, the last gym workout, the last trip to the guidance office – the conversations with many, seeing them again would be random and rare. Even those whom Nalu and his friends had never really cared for much, even they were treated with a slight bit of defference and respect. Not that they earned it, just out of lack of energy to harass or ignore them as they had for years prior. A gentle sadness slowly penetrated all around – even the after hours parties- some until the wee hours before dawn grew wilder and wearier to attend. Missed loves got conquered and quickly forgotten. Partying was rampant but lacked a joy that should have been there and wasn't.

33

Friday nights at the *Poly Room* on Banyan Drive got crazy and then crazier – alcohol blew through their systems as the legal drinking age was eighteen – and they were all that. Disco invaded Hilo Town, all the pretty girls were there! For some, fun was actually had and the dancing was late night exercise that almost kept them fit. For many, future bad habits were being formed rapidly that would morph into vices, divorces, addictions and worse. Faded time and corrupted energy on such a grand scale.

It's amazing how all of these things would cascade through them as groups and individuals – stacked choices would be tallied and counted – good versus evil and kind versus cruel.

Then the clock ticked to graduation day. Nalu wore board shorts and a nice white linen shirt under his gown. He had the traditional cap and tassel, he didn't get the special tassel – even though he had the highest IQ in his class – he looked at grades as more of a hobby than as a skill! Nalu liked to think of it as if he'd prefer to march with the 'tall guys' in the back of the column. He intuitively knew that A's and B's with little effort was a much better life for him, than all A's with tremendous effort ever would be. Why cram his brain with so much useless and ready to be forgotten trivia when it had nothing to do with his future plans? He was mostly right, but at times, incorrect. He liked to think of it as freeing up brain space for that which really mattered – surfing and babes!

Hawaiian graduations are extra-special in so many ways. There were the pick-up group of hula girls that did a traditional dance with non-traditional flare backed up with six of the guys pounding the floor with staffs of ohia and a lone *Taiko Drummer* [Japanses drums of thunder] sitting on the floor thundering a beat worthy of the gods.

One of the prettiest girls in the class, and on Earth for that matter, wore a full sleeve, full length *holoku* [elegant formal dress] of pure white with *maile* [fragrant green mountain vine] leis flowing, did a performance of such elegance and quality it made everyone old and young, frail and healthy, pagan and saint give a spontaneous standing ovation that could not be stopped. She exited blushing and astounded by the crowds spontaneity and cried herself as she sought her seat to listen to the featured speaker.

Mr. Earl *Shaka* Kimo Trask-Silva, speaker for the Class of Nineteen Hundred Seventy Six, was the love-hate science teacher. Fourth generation Big Island boy, Mr. Silva was one of the most difficult teachers ever; he taught at the utmost and beyond their levels as students. The marginal students he pressed relentlessly. The brilliant he pushed to such a degree that a love-hate relationship occurred as the years progressed and the rare genius among them – he prodded until they actually performed at the levels that they were capable of. Most for the first and only time in their educational experience.

Mr. Silva got the nickname 'Shaka' for obvious reason, he was missing his index finger and the two beside it, giving him the reality of a permanent 'shaka wave' with his right hand forever and ever. Students and life at times can be cruel, but, in this case it was such an obvious nickname that he simply went with the forces of the universe and did not ever fight the inevitable. He was a genius at most things, and the forces of gravity and observation were best left to his non-combative reality of being.

On the stage, in the center, dressed in black slacks and white shirt with a huge hanging to the floor maile lei of rich forest greens. Mr. Silva began, "Good evening distinguished guests, grandparents, parents of fortitude, friends of reknown, dreamers, visionaries, teachers, staff and those whom would choose to lead us. Lovers of all that is good, fitting and proper. And, yes, you the graduates, my favorite class – the class of seventy-six! Aloha from the very deepest part of my soul, my heart is on fire for you – for so many changes are coming at you unlike generations before.

"Most people simply know me as Mr. Shaka, of even simpler 'Shaka', yet so few of you even know how that name came about, or what is even in a name. GOD ALMIGHTY named me, along with my loving parents Earl Kimo Trask-Silva, but the events of a single night changed all of that to 'Shaka'. On a Saturday night, with way too much beer and contraband, with too much energy and not enough forethought – my life changed. At that time I thought life was over – how little wisdom was within me then.

"My two favorite uncles took me fishing outside of the breakwater – it was a dead calm night with just a sliver of moon and crosshatched swell from the east and the south, really not much, barely worth mentioning, just two to three feet. The ocean was like rippling glass and the stars bounced off of it as only they do in Hawaii Nei. We set a parachute of army surplus off of the bow to hold us flat in the current and proceeded to toss ika chum into the water a scoop every few minutes. We drank beer, told stories of marginal truths and then left some hand lines down hoping for ahi. Being the youngest and not as quick, not as ready nor as concerned as my uncles – mine was the last into the abyss that sits so close to here."

He looked up over his reading glasses, got even more serious and continued, "To this day I'm not sure if my line even hit the water, but what I am sure of is that a gorilla ahi hit with such velocity and with such force that it tore it out of my hands at great speed. Six hundred pound test line spooled out of the five gallon bucket between my legs and melted the flesh off of my fingertips faster than I could let go. Not accepting the obvious I reached to grab the line – not wanting to lose my trophy, not wanting to be ridiculed, but above all else, not being aware of my surroundings. I reached for six hundred pound test line with both hands that was flying out at the speed of sound, and that was a very bad mistake. That line threw a 'loop', snagged me around three fingers on my

35

right hand, and whipped me overboard so fast I never even got a single breath. I got pulled down into the ink black depths so fast and so far that I blew out both of my eardrums – it felt like someone had put two ice picks in both of my ears as they simultaneously exploded in pain. The only thing that hurt as much or more was the line as it slowly cut through my fingers; it stretched and sliced and stretched and sliced, and then I was suddenly free! I scratched my way back to the surface and air and life! I had just earned the name 'Shaka' forever and didn't even know it. All I knew was that air was the most important thing in the universe! Racing to shore, doctors, nurses and surgeons filled the next ten days of my life in an Oahu hospital – and my life would never ever be the same. You see until then I considered myself an 'artist' - for I loved to paint – but I loved the guitar even more; both of those loves were gone for good, and like a lost dream, soon bitterly forgotten."

Everyone there sat mesmerized by the story, from old to young. They all sat silent and stared at the man they thought they knew.

He went on, "what can we learn? What valuable lesson can be extracted and taught? Why in the world am I sharing this now? Here? On this stage? At this point in time?"

"Simply, because you must hear this, right now, right here and for reasons none of us – including me – will ever grasp or fully understand.

"Most major accidents occur because you make three errors in judgment in a row. One, two, three and you are dead. In my case – crippled."

'Shaka' looked out over his audience and very methodically went on, "First I had been partying, and impaired at a level that was unacceptable – that was the first mistake. Second, I had not been given, nor did I ask for, proper instruction, failing to recognize, although in an awesomely beautiful setting, how dangerous of an endeavor I was involved in and undertaking – that was the second mistake. And then, the fateful third mistake! The coup de gras, the icing on the cake, the fait accompli – I reached for the line! What in the world was I thinking? I, a scrawny kid with bare hands, was going to stop a two hundred plus pound ahi tuna on a death dive into the deepest and blackest abyss on Earth? Somehow, I was going to stop that! How arrogant and super stupid - beyond belief stupid! I knew better, but yet, obviously not!"

Then holding his crippled hand high overhead, "Let this sink in – one, two, three and you are dead! Flying, diving, surfing, hunting, fishing, sailing, driving, working or just plain walking – you will find this to be a universal truth as you go through life!"

He looked around, he had everyone's rapt attention, "Please be aware of your surroundings and also those surroundings of your loved ones that GOD

36

puts in your trust, as well of those strangers whom you don't even know. For Hawaii is famous for ocean, mountain and many other types of tragedies. Save whom you can in every instance.

"There is even one more truth – a much more important and universal truth from my experience – swim to the Light! Go to the Light – the Light of GOD. HIS Light will guide you home even from the darkest of realms, even in the coldest of depths, even in the most distant reaches of the human endeavor. HIS Light, however dim it may appear, will be the best choice, the only true guide, the warmest spot, and at times, your only hope to live."

"See the Light of CHRIST, call on HIS name and the pitfalls of life and this ever changing world laid before you will be, not only survivable but an absolute joy to behold!"

Shaka looked over the graduating class, and seeing only them, with a tear of both joy and pride, commanded them with tremendous force of a real heart felt aloha – "NOW GET OUT THERE AND DO SOMETHING!" [Emily G.]

The crowd went wild.

Diplomas were passed out, parents cried and grandparents beamed. Children laughed, everyone embraced until their mountains of leis were crushed with joy and tears. A misty soft rain came and went leaving a very well timed rainbow framing Mauna Kea above perfectly. Photos were taken in such abundance that an executive for Kodak woke up suddenly, for no apparent reason, five thousand miles away.

People, groups, and families slowly filtered out to various parts of the Big Island, the state, and the world at large.

So many, way too many, would never see each other again – they had been told this, but grasping it was beyond their experience – so it was of little impact or perception.

Finally a vacant lawn sat quiet, all had left except two lone figures folding chairs and hauling trash. The lawn was quiet, calm and moist from tears shed, memories folded into the past, amid bits and pieces of petals from the flower leis crushed into the green grass giving it the appearance of vibrantly colored living confetti that was soon to fade.

Nalu caught Samuel out of the corner of his eye as they traversed the parking lot and called out, "Samuel – where are you off to old friend?" smiling as he did it, sounding so proper and all.

"Three island tour starting tomorrow – going to make it to Poipu by sundown – gonna surf with my cousins on Kauai. Never surfed there, hear it's awesome!" Then he added, "You know – GOTTA GET OUT THERE AND DO SOMETHING!"

Everyone from both families laughed, smiled and got in their cars to leave.

Samuel caught Nalu's eye as they pulled out, held his hand out the window and above the car, then motioned goodbye with a wildly waving shaka.

Nalu returned the same - it was just for them - no one else caught it - no one else cared.

5

Samuel's Epic Journey - Part I

CITY OF HILO, ISLAND OF HAWAII

Samuel had had a fairly rough evening the night before. He'd been at the Poly Room with The Boys. Too much beer, way too much – but he'd met a fabulous young lady from Molokai of all places. She too loved horses and my-oh-my could she dance! She moved like liquid joy and had a smile that was magnetic. It melted him all the way through – he thought that maybe a trip to Molokai would be a wonderful expedition. Fishing was supposed to be awesome there as well.

He'd been jolted awake by his Auntie's ancient wind up alarm clock. He'd spent the night in her spare room sleeping on the futon she kept there for wayward nephews much like himself. Samuel found himself there on a regular basis – between school days at St. Joe and work on the weekends at Auntie Hula's, he'd hardly ever been home to see his parents and beloved Paint – he missed both tremendously.

His Auntie Em's house was older than she was – although both seemed to have one overriding characteristic – well preserved. The house was a single wall, tongue and grooved, square framed, 1,400 square foot plantation style, painted tin roof, exterior plumbing running over, up and around – all painted fairly recently an off shade of white. The miniature framings and the roof were painted as a trim in pale green. Although small, there was a quaint elegance about Auntie

Em's home. It fit neatly into this back street off Keaukaha – two blocks from the tidal ponds at Richardson Beach. One acre of meticulously groomed yard with gardens and fruit trees accented the small house in such a wonderful way as to be a setting fit for a master Japanese landscaper. Red, black, gold and green volcanic cinder and sand edged all aspects of the grounds. The fruit trees on the borders were of every known variety. Mangos of the Heyden variety were plump and juicy, smelled fresh and sat in a *koa* bowl on the counter, just picked from the yard.

Samuel grabbed one, along with his body surfing fins and the small bag he'd packed for his journey – one more reason to stay at Auntie's house; he had a flight to catch. *Aloha Airlines*, 6:05 a.m. to Kahalui, Maui. He'd won a stack of coupons in the Maui Hold-Em poker game a few months earlier, everyone used the coupons as twenty dollar bills, made it great for getting around the islands as and when needed, if you were winning. Having won them was extra sweet! He had two more tucked in his wallet. One to get to Oahu and then one to get on over to Kauai later in the day.

Auntie Em, huge as she was, came trotting out of her bedroom just then, "Samuel – you can not leave my home without a hug, my favorite nephew, now get over here!" She'd caught him just prior to him sprinting to the airport via his uncle's rusty, faded and shakey WWII era army surplus jeep sitting outside.

"Oh Auntie, thanks for letting me stay here one more time. Thanks for the mango!" He showed her the huge one he had in his hand. "Tell Uncle thanks for the jeep. I'll park it up in the grass as usual – save him from having to buy it out of the lot at the end of the day. And, Auntie, thanks for taking such good care of me this year while I went to school. It really saved me Auntie – and I love you for that and so many other things!"

Auntie Em melted, cried a little and then proceeded to squeeze him to crushing as only a 350-pound Hawaiian lady could do.

"*A hui ho* [until we meet again], Samuel – may GOD HIMSELF embrace you!"

Samuel leaped into the jeep, threw it in neutral, coasted it forward and prayed it would start. Seemed like every vehicle he was allowed to use had many issues – bad brakes, sloppy steering, broken shocks – but the one thing they all had in common was – it was always totally random if they were going to start.

The jeep fired up, the trip to the airport was illegally fast, he parked and sprinted to the gate, last one on the flight by seconds, and off to Maui! Climbing out he sat on the left side. Mauna Kea was awash in pale pinks as the sun illuminated its upper elevations and announced its presence to the Mid-Pacific -

calling her I am! Come rain on me clouds, for I shall stop your march and force you to pay today's ransom of watering my slopes with your tears and fog.

He saw Laupahoehoe pass by, just The Point though, for everything above it was shrouded in mist. He had a fleeting thought of Grace and looked for both her ranch higher up the mountain side and the white sand tidal pool, below, at The Point. He saw neither, which gave him pause and lingered at the edges of his mind as he tried to re-construct those memories. They seemed so long ago – before graduation.

Then the clouds parted. The sun was slightly higher and he caught an excellent aerial view of his family's ranch, Haiwiki – on the Kohala Mountains nestled in between two radiantly pink blue clouds. He thought of home and riding his favorite paint. Paint the Pony he'd named him when he was born, back when he was just a kid. He'd named him that, but after breaking him some years later, he graduated to simply Paint, a gelding of incredible agility, strength and style.

But then, Samuel thought of his parents, probably sitting at the koa counter in their ranch homestead drinking Kona coffee and talking without saying much of anything. Love transcends conversation.

Samuel silently said, "Goodbye Mom and Dad. I love you, and I hope to see you soon."

As they flew at 10,000 feet, over the Alenuihaha Channel so far below, he could easily see the swells doing epic battle with the current. Both could claim victory – the swells owned the surface, the current owned all other depths into the abyss and beyond. Cross-hatched lines ran from the west-northwest – an odd time of year for such a pronounced northern component. The cross-hatched portion was from the south-southwest and at times accentuated the wave action. Samuel could tell by the occasional monster sprays coming off of Upolo Point and the corresponding events on the eastern slopes of Maui's Haleakala.

It was a little lighter than it should have been outside, Samuel didn't realize that the gate agents had held the flight an extra four minutes just for him; something that he would never find out. Aloha wasn't just a name for the airline – it was a way of life and flowed all the way through it and many other island companies. After all, one never knew; Hawaii was such a small place.

Samuel glanced to his right and caught a little girl with huge blue eyes, specks of green within them and golden hair – somewhat unkempt and flowing everywhere – staring at him.

She asked matter-of-factly, "What are you?" Not so strange for a girl of her age.

Samuel, somewhat taken aback, responded with a gesture of hands to his chest, "I am a cowboy!"

She giggled and responded, "Cowboys are from Texas – that's what Daddy says." She gave him an x-ray look up and down, "And you are not from Texas. What are you?"

Samuel laughed and said, "Mexico is right next to Texas and there are cowboys there too. My great-great-great uncle came to Hawaii to be a cowboy for the great Hawaiian king – King Kamehameha. My family has always been cowboys ever since."

She rolled her eyes and said, "OK." Maybe not believing him, but not going to go any further.

Samuel laughed, then continued, "I love your flowers," pointing at her lei, "Those are pikake, my very favorite."

She leaned across the isle and said, "Smell them!" As she did so, and Samuel leaned in to get a closer whiff – she blew a huge blue bubble with her bubblegum, which exploded in his face. She laughed and giggled at his reaction.

Samuel couldn't help but notice the gum was vanilla and it mixed with the pikake to trigger the memory of Auntie Grace down at Laupahoehoe Point and her exquisite presence.

Samuel liked this girl wonderfully. What a beautiful firecracker! He thought he'd keep going, "Those are some really cool slippers. Did you get them here?"

"No silly, I brought them with me. Daddy said I could pack anything I wanted as long as it was for summer."

"I see your Daddy's sleeping. Where's Mommy?" Samuel immediately regretted his question.

The little girl got so sullen, instantly, "Mommy and brother Timmy are in Heaven. They died when that bad truck killed them. We are here because Daddy needed 'air'. I think he needed sleep. He's always so cranky anymore – not at me – but at everything else." She got very serious and continued, "Mommy is in Heaven, I see her and Timmy in my dreams. Daddy must not dream; he just cries."

Trying very hard to change the subject, Samuel continued, "I am so sorry. Have you ever been to Maui before? It is so pretty there. With that wild hair and cool slippers, I think my fine young lady, that you will fit right in!"

She smiled and simply said, "My name is Gracely." She had a bit of a lisp wrapped in an Appalachian accent. She meant to say Gracey – it just came out with an extra 'l' in it.

"Gracely – isn't that something?! The prettiest lady I've ever met is called Grace Lee, now the cutest girl I know is too!" Samuel was actually a little beside himself from the unexpected correlation.

"So what are you?" asked little Gracely once more.

"I am Samuel Kealoha, cowboy. But today I am a surfer that is hoping to make it to Kauai by this afternoon." He gave her his very best smile, held out his hand and said, "But you can call me Pancho."

She took his hand and said matter-of-factly, "I'll call you Samuel the Surfer – I'm still not sure you're a cowboy." She had made a decision, as many beautiful young ladies do, that not everything that boys tell them is true, and a Hawaiian cowboy would have to be confirmed by Daddy prior to belief.

To her, fairies and princesses and rainbow castles were more real, rang more true, than a Hawaiian cowboy could ever be.

"Samuel, can I surf?" she looked at him with ice blue eyes that went beyond normal existence.

"You'll have to be careful, and start with very small waves - but yes! Yes, young Miss Gracely, you can surf." Samuel gave his best and most positive tone and response possible. "And when you go in the water – stay close to Daddy until you get really really good."

"Daddy needs me; he's been so lost." She got this really deep thought and then her eyes flashed a magnificent color of green for a *nano-second* [smallest possible unit], then, as if from far off, "What he really needs is JESUS." She said it all so softly and so honestly.

Samuel was stunned and sat there taking it all in, then he blurted out, "How old are you?"

Gracely held up one hand full of fingers, "I am five, Silly, and that proves it! Girls are smarter than boys!"

She stuck out her tongue, puffed out her cheeks, made moose antlers with her hands and proceeded to blow a huge bubble that burst cheek to cheek, all at 'Samuel the Surfer'.

Samuel Kelaoha fell in love with a five year old girl in less than ten minutes time, on a crispy Hawaiian morning, as the flaps came out, the wheels came down and the approach was made across the isthmus of Maui on an Aloha jet. An early June morning sunrise enthralled those awake, but most of the state's population slept and the world didn't have a clue of what went on in the Land of Aloha.

* * * * * * *

KAHALUI AIRPORT, ISLAND OF MAUI

Samuel waited at the curb for his cousin of no relation, holding his wellworn pair of Churchill fins and his one hand-me-down bag, waiting to get a short surf session in prior to his 10:30 a.m. to Oahu. He knew that Kimo [James] would show up, wheels screeching – always in a hurry – perfect for this mission.

Then, from behind he felt a tugging at his *musubi* [rice ball] t-shirt, turning he had to look down.

"Well, hi again Gracely – how are you? Ready for Maui?"

"See Daddy – a real Hawaii surfer!" then she hugged him, super hugged around one leg and real gently, with great comfort said, "JESUS loves you Samuel the Surfer – look for HIS special dragonfly – it will be red."

Then she danced and skipped, caught her cool slippers on an uneven piece of sidewalk and almost went down only to be caught by her father's hand as they went around the corner. But of course, not before getting one last glance of Samuel standing there all shocked, sticking her tongue out, and blowing one huge blue bubble.

A soft, very warm rain, more of a whisper really, began to fall. Samuel barely noticed, it was the triple rainbow that had all of his attention.

Then what really got Samuel's attention was the overweight, dressed in a *Hilo Betty* twelve-dollar ultra-bright big flowered aloha blouse, very unaware tourist lady yelling at her husband to keep up. Then she ran over Samuel's foot with her steel wheeled luggage tearing his little toe nail completely off!

Samuel screamed. She gave him a look like it was obviously his fault and kept going. Never saying she was sorry, just barking at her husband to keep up or they'd miss the shuttle to the cheapest hotel on the island.

Samuel sat down on the curb, dislodged the final flakes of his destroyed toenail and tried not to cry. Blood flowed freely, and he stuffed the one lone napkin he'd kept from the onboard flight complimentary cup of Kona coffee around his newfound excruciating injury.

Of course, that is exactly when Kimo squealed to a stop beside him in a brand new Pontiac Firebird Trans Am, *Hertz's* finest. Kimo's father owned the Hertz franchise on the island and the entire family worked there. Kimo did also –

that is unless the swell was up, which was often, always a point of contention at the dinner table.

Kimo appraised his guest, "Wow brah! What happened to your toe?"

"Tourist woman, bad baggage skills, worse attitude." Samuel said, trying to be brave and not to cry in front of Kimo. Wow did it hurt, so much pain in such a small appendage!

Kimo said, "You'll live, swell's coming up fast, fluke swell – it's a double from the south and the northwest. Almost the entire island is breaking. I'm thinking Baldwin's since you've only got a few hours." Then looking at the blood and the fins, "Looks like we each have one fin now!"

In a minute they were half way out of the airport complex, in five minutes they'd hit 90 mph at least twice. Then, just before Paia Town, on the left, they whipped into Baldwin Beach park's entrance, pulled the emergency brake and did a *bat turn* [stunt maneuver] into a sand covered parking space.

"Does your Dad know how you drive these things?!" Samuel laughed, his mind no longer on his injured toe.

*   *   *   *   *   *   *

BALDWIN BEACH PARK, NORTH SHORE, ISLAND OF MAUI

"I hope not, look at those waves! Three feet solid, sand bar has to be bigger. What are you waiting for? DO YOU WANT TO LIVE FOREVER?!!" Kimo screamed over his shoulder as he raced with one of Samuel's Churchill fins at the sandbar shore pound going off like Krakatoa.

Glass conditions with perfectly formed eight-wave sets, then dead calm, coming across the sandbar – so odd for Central Maui. The sandbar was breaking at an oblique angle and into extremely shallow water. Each wave nearly perfect.

Kimo and Samuel caught wave after wave, then they would stand and chat in chest deep water between sets.

All was well with Kimo. His girlfriend had just dumped him again. Kimo had not learned one of the mysteries of the universe – girlfriends only wanted their boyfriends to have one, and only one, girlfriend at a time – what a concept!

Maui was a way too small an island to have more than one girlfriend – ever. Kimo didn't care. He was like Jesse on the Big Island; girls loved him. Each and every single one thought that they would be the one to tame him.

So far, they all had been incorrect.

"What is it with you, Kimo, girls everywhere, here, Oahu, Tahiti? Me – I've only got two. Both are absolutely gorgeous and both have the same name. Go figure! One is older and the other one is five – how strange is that?"

Kimo looked at him for a while, noticed he was absolutely serious and deadpanned, "Older's not so bad."

Samuel thought he said it with a little too much knowledge. So instead of dignifying his answer he dove across and threw him into a headlock and wrestled him on the sandbar – 'Aquatic Sumo' with a little 'Fu'.

Neither won. The next set of waves came and forced them to body surf, ending the modified wrestling match. Later both would claim victory.

Kimo glanced at his *Seiko* watch and longingly said, "Gotta go now if you actually want to make it to Oahu. Really? Honolulu on a Monday? You should stay here for a few days at least – surf's good, girls everywhere and you give me an excuse not to clean rent-a-cars. Some tourists actually treat them poorly. That's just wrong!"

He laughed, then they both just lost it, coming from Kimo it was rather rich.

Kimo caught a wave in and trotted towards the shower hidden in the ironwood trees.

Samuel was one set behind and that's when he saw them, two little kids going over the falls on a brutal shore pound wave. They'd gotten launched while holding onto their cheap Styrofoam board.

They couldn't have been any older than little Gracely on the plane.

Bad parents – what are they thinking?! Just then two flashes of color came down off of the sand, first the father than the mother a few feet behind. And that's when it got interesting. Both of them were frantic and got completely taken out by the very next wave. Four souls, an entire family, clueless and drowning on the perfect Hawaiian morning.

Multiple drownings, especially those involving whole families, were all too common. Hawaii news tried to downplay them and tended to bury the stories on the back pages, usually with almost no additional information or fanfare. Multiple drownings were very dangerous to the tourist industry, but lifeguards were so expensive – seemed like you just couldn't get around that darned minimum wage.

Samuel did not hesitate, he did not waver, and he simply grabbed the first handful of person underwater he came to. It was one of the children. He didn't know if it was a girl or a boy; he didn't care. He took four powerful kicks, launched the child in front of a rolling boil of whitewater and screamed, "Stand up and run!" They did, and he went looking for one of the other three. He saw the father come up with the other kid, flailing and choking, on his head. Samuel grabbed him around the chest getting two for one effort. Taking them both towards shore and on the back of the one breaking wave, he spoke way too forcefully into the dad's ear, "Go with me on this so you both live. I'll get your wife next, but you have to keep the kids on shore until I find her!" Then he rolled over, kicked the dad in the small of the back and launched him with the next incoming wall of whitewater. They made it and clawed their way up the sand to safety. Father, along with his two quivering children huddled on shore. The children were crying and then the father started pointing to Samuel's right. He was screaming, "There she is! I see her!"

Samuel heard nothing but concussions of the ever-increasing swell. Waves were going off all up and down the beach, but the one thing Samuel did was look right as he crested the next wave, and there, off to the right, was the wife - floating face down and she was not moving. Samuel sprinted the twenty yards over to her, swimming like never before! He grabbed her under the chin and rolled her over face up. He started swimming her methodically to shore. Timing was everything, and Samuel, with incredible timing, worked his lifeless charge through the wicked sets and landed her at the top of the wash line.

He rolled her over, did four quick chest compressions and then two quick breaths while holding her nose pinched shut. Boy was he glad that the nuns had made them all learn CPR. It dawned on him that it might have been the most useful skill he had ever learned.

Four more quick compressions, and before he could give her any more breaths, she sat up and promptly barfed all over him.

She lived, her family huddled under a towel together sobbing, and Samuel got up and slowly walked towards the showers. He really needed a shower. He was super-grateful to see a chunk of hotel soap wedged into the bracket holding the valve. As he showered, he noticed a little tiny iridescent dragonfly, sparkling green, hover around him, it did a complete lap – then stopped and looked right at him with those timeless, diamond glimmering bug eyes. What really startled him were the golden wings. That was just odd. Then in a flash, it darted off towards the temporary saltwater ponds formed in the depressions left from the high tide the night before.

Samuel grabbed his one lone fin and worked his way back to the cherry red Trans Am. Kimo was revving the engine and checking out the fresh and exciting new batch of tourist girls getting out of the jeep across the lot.

"What took you so long? I've got to get back to work, and you've got a flight to catch – it's important!" Kimo said half ticked, as he waved at the tourist chicks and blasted out toward the belt highway.

Samuel looked at the family still huddled under the beach blanket, looked up to Heaven and said very quietly and very sincerely, "Thank you JESUS, thank you."

Kimo was clueless. Samuel could not wait to get off of Maui. It was a bit too exciting for this early in the day – or summer - for that matter. He gave Kimo a high five, told him "thanks" and sprinted to the gate.

Exhausted he took a short nap on the flight to Honolulu. He dreamed of a huge wave bearing down on him and woke up with such a start that the lady sitting beside him gave him 'the look'. A look of; if you ever did something important, quit partying and actually got a real job, you may, just may, become a productive member of society. You loser! ……….. You surfer!

She conveyed all of that information in a single condescending glare of judgment.

Clueless tourist.

6

Samuel's Epic Journey – Part II

Uncle Jimmy, not a real uncle but a longtime family friend, picked Samuel up at the curb as he arrived at the inter-island terminal on Oahu. He was twelve years older than Samuel, but in good shape for being so old, and still loved to surf when he could. Jimmy had two older Town and Country boards with layers upon layers of wax on them in the back of his little Toyota pickup truck. He was recently married and working shift work down at the docks for *Young Brothers*. Nalu's father had 'helped' him get the job, now that he was married and all. Shift work, mostly nights, gave him time to go to school. He was taking business classes at U.H. at Manoa. He didn't know if he'd be able to get through four years, but some basic business classes would help immensely because he wanted to become a Real Estate Broker. Land values kept exploding across Oahu, and he'd read in the Hawaii Business Journal that four out of five new millionaires were making their fortunes in real estate.

And that is what Uncle Jimmy wanted, to become a millionaire, build a new house up in Tantalus for his new wife, raise children and, of course, surf when the waves were cooking – like they were today.

"Ready for some adventure?" asked Jimmy.

"Why not?!" Samuel answered having found a napkin in the glove box, as he did a fresh wrap on his throbbing toe.

"Uncle, where to?"

"I was thinking Point Panic. It's not too far and the swell is wrapping all the way around. I hear Sandy's is even breaking, but that's probably the trade winds," Uncle Jimmy responded, looking at Samuel. He added, "What's with the toe?"

Samuel filled him in on his exciting encounter with the obnoxious tourist woman at the curb on Maui.

Jimmy laughed, "How can you go through life so clueless? Must be from Southern California."

"Or Iowa," quipped Samuel.

"Or Kentucky," filled in Jimmy.

"Or," almost simultaneously, "Japan!" they looked at each other and just lost it laughing.

* * * * * * *

POINT PANIC, SOUTH SHORE, ISLAND OF OAHU

It was Hawaii in the early summertime, surf was up, and it did not get any better than this.

It was epic at Point Panic. Three standing tubes going off in synchronized formation. They had two hours and wanted to make the best of it. Although, Jimmy kept glancing at his watch, until Samuel finally asked, "What is it with the clock? I've got at least another hour."

Jimmy answered, "I've got to check in with work, not sure if I'm on or off tonight – and it's Kira's birthday."

"You ditched Auntie Kira [poetry in motion] on her birthday! For surf?" Samuel asked incredulously.

"She's working right now, but we either have a few hours at dinner time or all night if I can get off. Think I'll paddle in and use the pay phone back up in the parking lot. Do you have any change?"

"Here you go." Samuel found a few coins in his Velcro pocket – seemed like all of his buddies never had any money – at least not around him. Jimmy paddled in, and Samuel stayed for a few more sets, seemed he would have learned back on Maui that that's when things tended to get interesting.

50

And that is, of course, exactly when Samuel's world exploded. A young family in a rented speedboat making the turn way too fast and going for the channel, if it even was the correct channel, really screwed up. At an extreme excess of speed, the father, already drinking just like his wife was, blasted into the marked lanes and drifted wide past them and onto the reef, grinding the fiberglass bottom to nothing and shredding the coral heads as they came to an abrupt stop! Everyone, mother, father, and three children all flew against the starboard side and immediately launched onto the exposed reef being racked by white water from the surf.

Then the sets came and ate the boat a piece at a time; fuel spilled and the one still running engine ignited it. Concussions coming off of the resulting explosions are what really got Samuel's attention. He paddled over as quickly as possible and started gathering up the family.

Loading the now very sober mother and the two youngest onto the board – he, along with the father and the oldest son - slowly pushed the surfboard of dazed survivors towards shore.

First a tourist helicopter started circling the wreck, then a few moments later, much to their credit, a coastguard helicopter showed up on the scene with rescue divers. Appraising the spectacle, the jumper stayed on board the chopper and talked the pilot into a very tight landing spot just as Samuel the rescuer, and his surfboard of rescuees beached themselves on a tiny sliver of white sand.

KNZO's news helicopter was already there and got it all on film as a gaggle of *HPD* [Hawaii Police Depatment] escorted in the flashing and blaring land based Fire Rescue that came screeching into the park. Everyone's sirens announced their presence to the entire world.

It was a fiasco, but Samuel, the 'hero', took it in stride. The father was very embarrassed and he had a lot of explaining to do to both Fire Rescue and the HPD. Later on, he'd have to explain once again to the boat rental company and their insurance provider, which would prove to be even harder.

Young Samuel was fawned over by the KNZO news 'babe'. A local boy hero would make a good six o'clock news item and would easily be extended into the ten o'clock news hour as well.

KNZO's crew filmed the Fire Rescue EMS personnel bandaging his little toe. With a little prompting from the KNZO 'babe', they had the EMS girl bandage his whole foot.

She winked at Samuel, who sat there too embarrassed to explain that he'd been taken out by the luggage of a mad tourist woman. And, that it had happened on a completely different island.

Jimmy finally showed up, clueless, but ready to take Samuel back to the airport.

Samuel didn't say a word about what happened, he just asked, "Well Uncle, do you have to work tonight or is Auntie Kira in danger of having your attention for the entire evening?"

"Yea! Got the night off. Isn't that exciting?!" Jimmy answered as they raced to the Aloha gate so Samuel could make his early afternoon flight to Kauai.

Jimmy thought, hot date tonight!

Samuel thought, I hope Kauai is a little calmer. Man am I hungry; I'll eat that mango on the plane. Thank you, Auntie Em.

On the thirty-one minute flight to Lihue, Samuel sat quietly in his seat and ate his mango that he carved into slivers with his Swiss Army Knife that he kept in his bag at all times. He loved that knife, not for all of the cool gadgets, but for one gadget specifically – the toothpick – he used it to get the mango fibers out of his dental work between his upper left molars.

And that's when he saw it, at that exact moment in time, sitting directly in front of him on top of the seat back cushion which one more lost and confused tourist inhabited, a small, extremely delicate, golden-faceted eyes with see through golden winged, sapphire blue dragonfly.

"How in the world did you get in here?" asked Samuel maybe a bit too oddly and a touch too loud. " Hitchin' a ride to Kauai? Long flight for such a little fellow – over open ocean waters and all."

The dragonfly stared at him, and then, almost imperceptibly, looked longingly at his mango remnants.

"Care for a small piece? Only GOD knows how long you've been trapped in here waiting for me?" Samuel then offered a small piece of mango with a sliver of rind still attached. After all, who knows what portions of a mango a wayward hitchhiking dragonfly would prefer?

He held it up on the tip of the blade. The dragonfly, without hesitation, swooped in and plucked it with one fell snag. Then it buzzed off to points unknown on the Aloha jet traveling Mach .8 over the Kauai Channel far below.

How odd indeed; second dragonfly of the day and here of all places. Then, remembering his conversation with the fine young Miss Gracely, he thought, well at least neither of them have been red.

Samuel didn't even notice that he felt as good and natural about helping a stranded dragonfly as he did about the lives he'd saved earlier in the day – in fact he didn't even recognize it as such, just the way it should be – love first - without any elaborate plan, agenda or deep thought. Just a simple act of caring in an often brutal and dangerous world.

This time it just happened to be a lost, trapped and very hungry blue dragonfly on the journey of life, today, with him.

7

Samuel's Epic Journey – Part III

LIHUE AIRPORT, ISLAND OF KAUAI

Kauai was the real objective all day and Samuel was totally excited to actually arrive. As he disembarked the plane - his newest best friend - the dragonfly buzzed past his ear to freedom. It was still clutching a tiny piece of the mango as he flew by. It made Samuel smile.

Samuel looked at his overly bandaged foot and started to unwind the bulk of the strips that were entirely unnecessary. His cousin, twice removed on his mother's side, was picking him up to give him a ride to their home for the summer. It was near a guava farm that trained and rented horses on the side, mostly to tourists, but it was such an awesome location being in Hanalei Valley, even by island standards, that many locals came from all of the islands to ride as well.

This summer job would give Samuel time to enjoy Kaui Nei, spend time with Kulei [beloved], one of his most favorite people in all of the world, and become familiar with Kaui's horses, ranches and such. Also, he'd heard, that the surf could often be beyond epic on Kauai – even the south and west shores in the summer could get big at times.

Little did he know what an isolated island, devoid of the wave shadows cast by other islands nearby, could offer in the way of open ocean swells.

Kulei came freewheeling into the airport in a tattered, rusted and smoking Chevy Blazer – hopped out with it barely stopped – leaped across and hugged Samuel all the while smiling from ear to ear. Kulei, with great enthusiasm said, "Ready for some epic bodysurfing? West End is huge and Barking Sands is making the beach dance with its clean up sets! And, by the way, this is Kimi [free spirit] and Noe [beautiful one]– they will be keeping the beach safe while we brave the waves."

Kulei threw his arm around the tall long legged babe of a blonde with the cut off jeans and the t-shirt tied to the side, "This one's mine!" Giving Kimi a kiss on the cheek, he whooped Samuel's bag into the back through the window that hadn't been there, obviously, for some time.

"Noe, this is Samuel. Samuel this is Noe. She is yours if she'll have you. OK, you two in the back! Kimi, you're with me. Shotgun!"

Kimi and Kulei laughed with wild abandon. Samuel and Noe were a little too embarrassed to laugh. Both blushed and quietly crawled into the back seat of the hammered Blazer.

It was one wild ride to the southwest corner of Kauai, and was as life threatening as anything Samuel had experienced all day. The very best aspect about the ride was Noe snuggled into his side, without asking, just as natural and wonderful as could be. She was intoxicatingly cute, and Samuel was smitten and at a total loss for words.

America played on the cassette tape player, tunnels of green umbrella trees folded over the road above. Kimi and Kulei sang along with the tape, inserting *'Kauai'* instead of *'Ventura'* as they adlibbed and thought that the entire world was theirs. Noe made Samuel feel like a prince – allowing all of the hurts and pains to evaporate. Life on Kauai was already much more and so much better than he had ever imagined. Samuel breathed in the air ripping across his face, held Noe a little tighter, and got lost in the moment of bliss that engulfed him.

Noe might just be 'the one'. Some events in life are so obviously right that deep thoughts and rational conversation are unworthy of contemplation – the reality of the moment is all that matters.

Kulei glanced in the rear view mirror, turned it down a little, saw his favorite cousin with his nicest classmate and thought, mission accomplished!

* * * * * * *

POLIHALE STATE PARK, NORTHWEST SHORELINE, ISLAND OF KAUAI

In one fell move, Kulei smiled at the gangly, wind swept blonde beside him and lurched on the steering wheel to the left towards Barking Sands, better

55

known on the map as Polihale State Park. But all surfers simply called it Seven Miles.

Seven miles of sand dunes, powder sand, golden hues, white fringes, dripping green cliffs with red dirt outcroppings. Lobsters in the summer and surf when you couldn't go diving. What a location! South of Na Pali – the wildest and most untamed valley system and ocean seacliffs in the state, and the world for that matter.

Of course Samuel thought the same about the Hamakua and the Seven Valleys Of The Kings. After all, you could put the entire Island of Kauai in that single portion of the Big Island, but why argue about facts?

After all, The Seven Valleys Of The Kings didn't have Noe.

Seven miles of golden sand shaped, molded, pounded and crushed by the largest open ocean stretch of water on Earth. Barking Sands Missile Range – protector of the great western corridor and the first line of defense for any western launched missile attack against the USA. A base of operations for man, but created by GOD. This area was carved by the CREATOR's hand with the long beach being the gateway to the cliffs of Na Pali. Inaccessible and remote seacliffs carved from relentless rains, huge ocean swells and forces of old before time, or the current age of man, was a consideration.

One hammered and nearly defunct old Blazer pulled up about half a mile from the far end, stopped right at the edge of the sand and disembarked four intrepid souls. One long legged filly of a blonde with her six foot one local boy surfer, farmer and second year UHH student – both looking like perfect specimens of a new and brave world of interracial cooperation. Two more - one scrawny Hawaiian cowboy of tremendous vigor made from spring loaded steel with a great awareness about him and his new found joy, an unbelievably cute, tight, fit, soft spoken child of GOD that had the ability to have a raging crowd go dead silent with a single glance, smile and swing of her belt length hair.

Kimi, Kulei, Noe and Samuel controlled the environment wherever they chose to be, but at this spot on Earth they simply blended. Na Pali was intoxicatingly wild with seven miles of golden sand carpet laid out like a doormat for the thousand foot towering mountain edges dripping with out-croppings of myriad shades of black, brown and red rocks permanently dressed with waving variations of green flora climbing into the clouds above. All pushed, prodded and sculpted by six thousand miles of relentless ocean forces.

And, wilder yet, you could occasionally catch a missile launch aimed at phantom enemies at random times! Doesn't get any better than that!

Noe took off her *sarong* [single piece wrap] to use as a beach towel and laid it delicately at her feet exposing her lime green bikini, totally uniform deep light chocolate tan and the fact that she was drop dead cuter than ever. She smiled; Samuel gasped.

Seeing the interchange between them, both Kulei and Kimi just lost it, laughing at the two friends' awkwardness.

Hooting and hollering, The Boys sprinted to the ocean shore-pound below, not mindful of the huge whitewater getting tossed against the seacliffs half a mile away at the far right point. They weren't surfing out there anyway. The shore-pound was only three to four Hawaiian measurement style but still very unusually large for this time of year. Summer swells shouldn't be here, strange for June, especially with such large western and northern components.

It was four in the afternoon, or thereabouts, and the waves were heavy for their size and seemed to be endless with no lulls – just set after set after set.

The girls chatted, giggled and tanned, doing all three exceedingly well.

The Boys caught wave after wave after wave. With lots of beach to use never really worried about staying where they were in the water or fighting for position. They allowed the *sideshore current* to slowly carry them towards the far end of the beach, gradually putting ever-increasing distance between them and their companions. It was a leisurely day of play on an island paradise.

Yet, there are always those who can screw up anything, and events beyond human control can be the catalyst that can turn paradise into a disaster zone, just like the missile launches – random and unannounced seemed to be the only schedule they ever knew.

Exactly at that moment is when the red rent-a-Mustang with the top down and the family of five showed up. It must have taken some spectacular driving to get it back into this far section of Barking Sands and one highly motivated driver.

Five souls promptly leaped out of the car and proceeded towards their doom. They didn't have a clue of their surroundings and their ocean skills and awareness factor were even less.

Tourists! Covered in oil from all points of the Earth – trying to enjoy that which can't be tamed, and at this exact spot they chose to descend upon one of the wildest sections of shoreline on planet Earth, happy as could be and barely able to swim. Actually only four out of five could. The youngest, being only three, had zero water skills. Her older siblings could swim about the width of a medium sized swimming pool on a good day.

Simultaneously, about two hundred yards away, Samuel and Kulei got caught in a rare phenomena themselves, the endless parade of wave sets simply stopped. Artificial surge, tide and inflation of the long stretch of beach in the correspondingly large bay caused it to be a few feet higher tide than the ocean itself. That bay now was free to drain, and it drained with hydrodynamics that caught Samuel and Kulei by total surprise. The sideshore current rapidly increased and moved them towards the far north end at speeds approaching seven knots and swept them further from shore. All of this happened silently and with little notice by them until the babes they'd left sunning, quickly became specks of brown and blonde on the beach far away.

They never saw it coming, none of them. The five tourists of Japanese variety simply set up their gear. The girls were just now having it dawn on them that their guys were far away, even worse, they were rapidly disappearing! And The Boys themselves now knew that forces beyond their control had grabbed on to them. All of a sudden, things spiraled into the danger zone.

Mr. Fujitani [trustworthy, honorable, worthy], along with his wife and three children, had just gotten past the worst of their jet lag, having flown in from Osaka a day earlier. He'd recently been promoted in the family owned and run business that delivered natural gas to the vast majority of Osaka's households and industries. His family employed over 5,000 and owned the largest skyscraper in the heart of the city. He and his family lived on the top five floors. He was ghost white, having never enjoyed anything but a fluorescent tan most of his adult life. His wife, Yuriko, had been 'designer engineered' by the family and their related *Keiretsu* just for him. They made a lovely couple. She asked few questions and gave him three wonderful and lively children. He gave few answers and treated her with the utmost respect when, and if, he was home. Theirs was the modern version of the ancient arranged marriage, which kept the family dynasty intact. For Mr. Fujitani, running the family enterprise took tremendous effort and all of his waking hours.

But today, whatever day it was, was perfectly awesome – they got a cool American car and headed down the highway – immediately got lost, and then, saw this road to the far end of what appeared to be the perfect beach. Perfect – that's how it should be!

Yet, worlds collide, cultures clash, and events can overtake blue skies and golden sands.

Samuel and Kulei hit the sandbar at the same time. Both stood up in ten inches of water just a few feet apart.

"Never saw anything like this Kulei!"

"Me neither! Whatever you do – don't go past this sandbar! Look at that rip; it's a raging river to oblivion!" Kulei shouted back – pointing at the largest *rip current* [fast current moving away from shore] either of them had ever seen. That rip current ran along the far cliff face and was over one hundred yards wide. It was super saturated with sand, making it ultra heavy dark brown, raging with rapids in a very well defined journey to the *cloud breaks* [massive waves] going off in the far distance at the point which was the gateway to the ocean wilderness beyond.

Water blew up their legs and fanned out off of their backs as they both fought for position and tried to remain standing. They were watching the ocean eat the sandbar they were stuck on. A few more minutes, and it would not matter one way or the other. The sandbar was actually dissolving under them as the entire seven miles of bay swept it toward the rip current, now just fifty yards away.

They both just looked at each other and without a word they knew – wrong place, wrong time, wrong stretch of ocean.

Then an intervention from the ocean itself – the sets came back – bigger than before. Now they found themselves at the second break and instead of the waves being the smaller three to four shore-pound, it was six to eight 'Hawaiian style'. The wave sets were once again relentless. Neither tried to body surf. They both just leaped up and into the oncoming walls of whitewater and took the beatings. But those poundings eventually pushed them toward shore; two more and they were flushed up onto the sand. They were dazed and fatigued, but safe from harm - surviving, barely, and not having been eaten by the sea that had gone crazy.

And, of course, that's when the tourists decided to take a family picture! Mr. Fujitani lined up his wife and three children down by the water to get one for the album. He was waiting for the perfect huge whitewater splash for background effect. After all, he was Japanese and photography and cameras were in his blood.

That last picture ever taken with his brand new *Olympus* 35mm camera had one huge splash for a background – bigger and better than Mr. Fujitani could have ever hoped for. That same huge splash swept all five of them into the water! First it seemed uneventful. Just a sheet of water running through their legs with warmth they'd never expected. Then they started dropping like dominoes as it took their feet out from under them and pulled them one by one into the surf zone that had a crushing hydraulics all its own.

Samuel saw the event first, and once again rose to the occasion. What a day! Couldn't he just save himself for once? Good Heavens!

So totally exhausted and running on a non-earthly charge of adrenalin, he sprinted to the location where the family had been, grabbed the lid off of the cooler they'd brought with them and used it as a make-shift Boogie Board to start his impromptu third search and rescue of the day.

59

He immediately found the three-year-old, upside down, feet sticking toward the sky, then he swam her back to shore. It only took a few seconds since a wave was right there. Samuel pointed at the beach gear they'd brought and sent her that direction. Back out to the rest of the family, now scattered and in various stages of panic. He gathered up the two remaining children and put them on the lid, floating them just outside of the massive shore-pound going off like thunder. He saw their mother in extreme duress and worked them altogether toward her. With three on the lid, he had to swim beside it since the buoyancy was now at peak performance. Slowly he worked them against the current, ever wary of the sandbar looming not so far away and the doom just beyond it. Seeing an opportunity to launch them towards shore, he did it with exquisite timing. The wave exploded, depositing three very distraught Japanese tourists at the top of the wash zone – together, uninjured but disoriented. They all had sand in places they never knew sand could get to.

Mr. Fujitani was having his own issues. Not only had he been crushed by six consecutive waves, his Olympus camera had done a double wrap around his neck and left arm. He was drowning and flailing and drowning and flailing and drowning and eating sand laced water through his mouth, nose and ears. None of it was he doing gracefully. For Mr. Fujitani, this was the end!

Samuel, once more, charged the shore-pound and caught sight of the distressed, floundering father just as they both hit the sandbar. Samuel tore off the camera and ditched it, picked him up as the water flew past and threw him into the oncoming whitewater. Then he did it again and again – picking him up after each wall crushed by. Finally he saw an opportunity, gave Mr. Fujitani a quick shaking to get his full attention, wrapped his arms around the cooler lid, and sent him toward shore and beyond the reach of the sets, which once again had turned relentless.

Kulei and the girls watched all of this take place; the girls comforted the mother and children, Kulei said nothing as he looked at his folded over right leg beneath him. He had a compound fracture and was bleeding way too much. He'd broken it in two places when he went back out to assist Samuel during the rescue! On the very first wave he'd encountered! After that he barely survived himself, as he crawled up the beach and slowly descending into his own world of shock and shattered dreams.

Mr. Fujitani was reunited with his entire family. On a lonely stretch of beach by a young man he would have treated with total disdain just minutes earlier. A *gaijin* [barbarian] being hardly worthy of acknowledgment or notice. He now owed that gaijin the biggest debt one could ever owe anyone and never possibly repay. Mr. Fujitani was overwhelmed with emotions and could not process them.

Samuel could care less about Mr. Fujitani's internal conundrum and his confused *Samurai* [honorable noble warrior] sense of duty. Samuel didn't make it off of the correct side of the sandbar this time. He was swept into the raging rip current and was well on his way to finding out just how massive the cloud breaks at the far point really were. He was so fatigued and had lost his one remaining fin! He didn't know where, all he knew was that he felt very naked and vulnerable as he negotiated the raging currents he'd been thrust into by events bigger than he.

Kulei called to Noe and Kimi and said, "Go call Air Rescue! DO IT NOW! It's getting darker by the minute! GOD, I hope they are somewhere near this side of the island. They're Samuel's only hope at this stage!"

*　*　*　*　*　*　*

HAIWIKI RANCH, KOHALA MOUNTAINS, ISLAND OF HAWAII

Four hundred miles to the east, on a heavenly stretch of a sliver of the Kohala Mountains, Samuel's parents had calmly put away the days chores and settled into their evening routine. The sun was casting an awesome display of pale pinks with hues of gunmetal blues as the lime green hills danced in their glory above them.

Mr. Kealoha [the love] made a fire out of fallen ohia branches in the fire pit ringed with round beach rocks that he'd gotten from Pololu Valley years ago. With the coals, he positioned four bricks in a rectangle and placed a recovered Weber grill grate upon them. Since it was just the Missus and him, he took one porterhouse steak cut thick from that year's beef steer and threw it on the 'country' grill. Having dusted it in Hawaiian Sea Salt, crushed chili pepper from the garden bush, and fresh ground pepper. He had thawed it on the counter earlier in the afternoon for this evening's meal. He loved that chili pepper bush, when he'd get some mainlander in wanting him to do this or sell that, he'd ask them, "Have you ever tried our Hawaiian cherries?" real nonchalantly. He had had one old geezer that was especially obnoxious, actually sprint into the house and spit his false teeth into the sink and consume mass quantities of water directly out of the tap trying to quench the fire in his mouth!

Seemed like an appropriate time to introduce him to the Missus, while he spit and gargled for air. He thought it was hilarious – the Missus, not so much!

The Kealohas settled in for a quiet and charming evening's dinner. Once again the conversation was nonexistent for the better part of the meal. It was a simple meal with salad from the garden. She got the fillet portion of the over-sized steak, he got the strip portion and the older-than-dirt Dogg got the bone with lots of scraps on it.

All was well on the ranch as the sun kept marching toward the sea far to the west.

She went first voicing what they both were thinking, "Think Samuel made it to Kauai? Wonder how his day went? Hope the flights actually flew and the cousins were there and didn't leave him stranded in the airport. And, Father, did you see how Paint the Pony's been acting this evening? Standing straight as a statue on that little knoll over there – I'd swear he's looking due west at Kauai – if I didn't know better!" She gathered up the minimal dishes then proceeded toward the sink, "I'd think that horse misses him more than we do – if that were possible."

* * * * * * *

POLIHALE STATE PARK, NORTHWEST SHORELINE, ISLAND OF KAUAI

Noe and Kimi blasted to the nearest Mom-N-Pop store, burst into the place, ran behind the counter without asking and called fire rescue. Gave an impassioned plea, got assurances, then headed at a way-too-fast high rate of speed to get back to Kulei. They had made him a sand chair and left him with the Fujitani family. Kulei was trying his best to remain conscious and not look at his shattered and twisted leg, all the while looking for any signs of Samuel. To this point in time, there were none. Just his lone Churchill fin that occasionally came and went in the whitewash, floating tip up, and of no use to the one person that needed it desperately.

The Fujitani family sat with Kulei. No communication was occurring, after a few dismal starts and failures, the efforts were better left unsaid. The entire family forlornly scanned the horizon together. What they expected to do if they spotted Samuel was yet to be determined. One overriding thing Mr. Fujitani had going was the immense and deep sense of guilt and shame cascading through him for being the cause of this event.

Kulei looked at him and thought – good thing that guy doesn't have his sword with him; I'm afraid he'd fall on it and make an even bigger mess.

Yet, when the Fujitanis looked at him, he simply bowed his head in acknowledgement. After all, how would they have known that such an epic saga as this would invade their cloistered and pristine world?

Samuel was in the process of fighting his own epic battle, which didn't involve pondering deep emotions. It was an unmitigated struggle for existence!

Things got bad … …

Then really bad … …

Then they got worse to the infinite!

62

NA PALI COAST STATE PARK, NORTHWEST SHORELINE, ISLAND OF KAUAI

Samuel found himself standing on a ledge that was about eighteen inches wide and about seventy feet off the water. That guesstimate, the height portion, was totally in flux as the swells beneath him came and went.

He'd made it through the cloud breaks, by far the largest waves he'd ever ever experienced. Huge waves blowing overhead as he dove down into the 'safe zone', calmer water that kind of existed between the reef and the boiling white water above. He did it time after time until he'd been forced around the corner and out in front of the towering cliff, the beginnings of Na Pali, and into the shards of exposed slivers of lava rocks guarding the entrance.

Na Pali's cliff entrance section was way wider than he'd hoped and trying to conserve his remaining energies he'd attempted to cut the corner hoping the beach landing was not too far away.

It was a strategic error, which provided little recourse or forgiveness.

One huge wall of foaming mass pushed him onto a shelf. Being fully exposed he took the only way out. He climbed up and away from the raging waters. Getting out of the water was a great thing, where he found himself, not so much. For that is how he found himself here – treed by an angry ocean – standing on a sliver of shattered and broken splinter of a rock. Samuel was on an eighteen-inch wide ledge, high upon a towering shard that looked like a broken piece of an ancient Damascus Steel Blade created by the hand of GOD tearing it away from the thousand foot cliffs behind him.

If he hadn't been quivering from current circumstance, he'd be awestruck by the beauty that enveloped him at every side. Waves boiled, rolled and exploded upon the cliff faces behind him, having been split by the very knife-edge he stood on. Those same cliffs stood majestic against the raging waters and said, "Here you go and you shall go no further!" The waves answered by courses of thunder cast all about and in their backwash and mists that pushed hundreds of feet into the air creating rainbow after rainbow that encircled Samuel on his perch of a vantage point.

The rainbows came and evaporated then appeared again as Samuel slowly regained his strength and composure. He was a child of the mountains and the sea – so gradually the fears subsided and he grasped not only where he was, but also, what he was. For the ocean and the rhythm of its living waters ran in his bloodstream and he would not be dismayed.

An awesome sunset burst to the west, creating the most beautiful effervescent atmosphere, everything went liquid pink as the mists came and went. At this time is when he saw it. The ocean, for the second time in one day, gave up one more of her secrets. An event of lore and legend – rarely ever seen by mortal man - talked about, mostly in whispers, by old fishermen given by hand-me-down stories passed from generation to generation.

Samuel, looking down, saw the floor of the ocean disappear into the abyss before his very eyes! For the ocean pulled away from the shoreline, the sand that remained on the shelf below, simply fell into the labyrinth of lava tubes below and everything disappeared into the abyss in unison.

The very floor of the ocean dissolved into oblivion!

That visual sight triggered a long distant memory, told by his great-uncle at the campfire on an overnight ulua fishing journey down at a place they called 'The End Of The World' near South Point on the Big Island. He had been only seven years old and that was his very first overnight camping experience. It seemed that the older guys – late at night – liked to spook the youngsters with tall tales of goblins. But those were not the really scary stories. The really really scary stories were the ones based in truth, wrapped in legend and accented by fire light, with an emphasis on those who didn't come home.

What Samuel remembered from this memory was that when the 'floor falls out of the bottom of the ocean', the ocean was hungry. *Rogue waves* [monstrous waves previously thought mythical, now proven scientific fact] were just over the horizon looking for souls to feast upon and shorelines to wash away.

Sometimes the legends of days long past are salted with truth – truth that can only be ignored at your own peril.

Taking stock of his surroundings, Samuel saw one lone keiki ulua trapped in a tiny pool of water right there in front of him at the tip of the shard. That's when the reality of the situation really sunk in. That baby ulua was healthy; some wave had recently deposited him here, seventy feet off of the water line!

And that singular fact was not good.

Samuel scooped the panicked fish and carefully tossed him underhand into the lesser raging waters below. By doing so, he realized that the seacliffs had been undercut by relentless ocean swells over centuries of time, and had various caves pockmarked into them. Some were small, about three feet or so across. At least three caves were much bigger with just the tops visible when the swells sucked out and allowed a viewing. They were at least thirty feet or more across – those sections of the massive ocean cliff bases were sure death.

Both to his left and to his right it was not any safer. They had table rocks that looked like liquid cheese graters. He was in the only place he could possibly be and survive. Man, he hoped to have made it around the corner, but it was not to be. Spending the night on this tiny ledge was starting to seem like the only rational option that would allow him to see a new day.

Looking out to sea, he scanned the horizon hoping for just a tiny bit of good news, a tiny piece of hope, a sign that he would get home to Mom and Dad. Home to ride Paint. That he would have at least one real date, without all of the drama, with Noe; and be able to get some Spam musubi from his favorite little store in Hawi Town along with a new pair of Churchill fins.

Just a single shred of hope would be great.

He put his head down for a moment, both in sheer exhaustion and deep reverence. He crossed himself spontaneously, without thought of the act, and he said to the wind and the waves, "Jesus! Here I stand! I am now and forever have been Yours, please do with me, Samuel Kealoha, as You will."

He heard an immediate buzzing over his shoulder. Turning he saw the deepest red dragonfly, it was huge, had golden faceted eyes and golden translucent wings that stopped as it alighted on the very tip of the rock shard directly before him only inches away from his face.

Then the dragonfly looked over Samuel's shoulder, lifted up to a hover just off his side. Together the blood red dragonfly and Samuel looked at the horizon as shadows of huge waves came and went from view.

Rogue waves of immense proportions were on the march! Like battalions of warriors with a wicked agenda they lurched forward, resetting the ocean depths, allowing the pushing current to once again dominate the strait between Kauai and the Forbidden Island of Niihau far off in the distance that at this stage cast a silhouette in front of the setting sun.

Huge cathedrals and columns of light burned through portals above, danced upon the surface of the sea and all along the fading mountain peaks off in the distance.

As the sets approached, the dragonfly spun around, looked Samuel in the eyes, and, catching an updraft, hovered straight up being illuminated by the lone shaft of luminescence that spotlighted Samuel's plight.

Samuel gazed up and caught a final glimpse of the dragonfly lit up like an angel far above. And that's when it hit him - the words Gracely had spoken earlier in the day! How in the world would she know to tell him this very event so many hours earlier? It felt like decades ago, for he had been such a younger man at that time.

The first rogue wave of the set was parted by the shard he stood upon. It passed just below his feet and exploded with such force against the seacliff behind him that he was afraid the violent recoil concussion would tear him from the rock!

He didn't need to fear any such turn of events. With the sheet of rebounding water flowing back around his shard, the second wave lifted skyward and was far bigger. So rather than getting 'peeled', he dove with great elegance, poise and as much strength as he could possibly muster, all the strength he had remaining, directly into the gaping jaws of the top of the monsterous and towering wave breaking upon him.

* * * * * * *

HAIWIKI RANCH, KOHALA MOUNTAINS, ISLAND OF HAWAII

Four hundred plus miles to the east Paint the Pony let out a snort and did figure eights in the paddock as an extreme and sudden downburst of rain let loose on the ranch.

That sudden burst of rain cascaded off all the roofs, including the small ranch hand's cottage near the *mauka* [up mountain] side of the main house. It had been hand built over thirty years earlier by a Japanese artisan who spoke zero English, ever, in his lifetime. Mr. Tanaka-*san* was gifted and had hand pieced the cottage together without using nails. All the work was accomplished with dovetail joints and wooden pins that held the koa and *sugi pine* structure together. The roof and the gutter were of fine patina copper with downspouts of woven copper chains discharging into the gardens of pikake, orchids and ginger that graced the house with their beauty and fragrance.

Yet the oddest feature of all was probably not of Japanese origin. It was the cast bronze bells tied together and wrapped around the western chain downspout. When it rained just right, like it was at this very time, they sang an ancient melody, a chorus of angels – a lullaby really - that drifted into the main house and resonated across the ranch with a touch of their divine whispers from Heaven.

8

Samuel's Epic Journey – Part IV

THE REALM

An indeterminate amount of time went by for Samuel. He'd managed to swim through the wave, and as he did so, three huge concussions blew through him at a primal level and he found himself floating, once again, in the 'safe zone'. He saw huge billows of foam pushing down from above and a shifting bottom blurred out in deep green that was below him.

Then he saw it, a tiny glimmer of light far to the outside, so he started swimming toward it. As far away as it was, he still had just enough air to reach it. It was out of the chaos that engulfed him and was his only hope.

Breaking the surface he got a huge gulp of fresh air and did not grasp his surroundings at first.

Then he heard from over his right shoulder, "Here – grab my hand!"

Looking up he saw a bronzed Hawaiian man smiling like the noonday sun and with glistening white hair. He could be forty or sixty. He looked amazingly fit and grabbed Samuel's outstretched wrist, and Samuel grabbed his. He flicked Samuel into the bow of the two-man *outrigger* canoe of ancient design and pristine condition.

Samuel laid on his back against the bow and gazed at the magnificent individual before him, that man calmly announced, "Hello Samuel – I am Gabriel."

It did not seem strange that the ocean was calm and clear as glass. It did not seem strange that all was aglow with a radiance that seemed limitless and without origin. The only thing that seemed odd was how good he felt. Samuel felt wonderful, rejuvenated and strong – that's what felt so strange. Because with that third thundering concussion, he'd been so weary and lightheaded, and that was just moments before.

Now he felt great!

Powerful strokes of the paddle propelled them towards a goal that Samuel couldn't see. Gabriel motioned to a second paddle beside where he lay. Samuel turned, picked it up and got in rhythm with his one-man rescue party.

This stretch of ocean was alive! Fish, schools of them, were everywhere. Two spinner dolphins rode just before them on the mini bow wave. Birds, huge flocks of them, soared past overhead, and then he saw it – one lone blood red dragonfly with golden eyes and wings sitting into the wind on the strut of the outrigger on his left.

With calculated risk, and not wanting to offend in any way, Samuel asked, "Gabriel – where are we?" almost afraid of the answer that was coming.

"Welcome to The Realm, my dear hero of a friend. Welcome to The Realm! This is the Third Heaven – the abode of GOD ALMIGHTY. Congratulations - you have made it." He continued, "I've got someone who is waiting to see you. She anxiously awaits your arrival, as many others do as well."

Then in very solemn tones, "HE is waiting for you. HE personally sent me for you. It was an honor to have that privilege, my dear friend."

Light permeated all around. No shadows discolored the lush hillsides. The ocean was clear with a tinge of liquid gold, trees with fruit of new varieties lined the shore. It was literally too much to take in or process. In fact, he may never be able to grasp the depth, the beauty, and the otherworldly qualities of what so willingly embraced him. He got lost in the beauty that washed away the cares of the far distant world from which he'd just come. Hawaii Nei, for all of its' qualities, held not even a reflection of The Realm. This place called Heaven.

They stroked the little outrigger canoe for an indefinite amount of time. Finally they turned into a stretch that appeared to be a well defined river, flowing through orchards of umbrella trees and fruit trees, stands of immense timber and open grasslands with snow capped peaks – layers of peaks far off to the distant horizon.

Grasslands came and went. Through it all, they paddled without a word being spoken, just a deep radiating love of kindness that knew no language, nor did it need to, for love speaks a simple volume of joy that desires few words.

"We are here, Samuel. I've been given strict orders to take you straight away to meet up with your friend first. There she is under that lone tree on the far side of the River Of Life." Gabriel smiled, pointed and said, as he beached the canoe, "Thank you, Samuel Kealoha, it was without a doubt one of the highlights of my day to see you here. Aloha and welcome to the Living Now."

Samuel took that as his clue to disembark. Pushing the bow around, he re-launched Gabriel to points unknown. He seemed to evaporate into the distance almost immediately. Turning around, he was so startled that he was shaken absolutely speechless.

"How in the world?!" Samuel gasped, looking at Noe standing before him radiating beauty and poise with a smile that stunned him to his core.

She said nothing, simply walked up to him, kissed him on the lips very delicately, and tucked herself under his arm with one sweeping gift of sincere joy to see him.

Then, looking him in the eyes, she said, "It appears that HE wished for us to meet at least once on Earth prior to being called home to HIM - and my dear Samuel – I beat you here. That alone proves that girls are smarter than boys!"

They both hugged and then came completely unglued, laughing. The burdens of Earth no longer existed.

Such is Heaven – such is The Realm of the LIVING GOD.

9

Tremendous Loss

From the moment the bells started singing on that Monday evening in June, they would sing without stopping for exactly seventy-two hours, then they would abruptly stop along with the falling rain.

No one would be there to notice – no one would be there to care.

* * * * * * *

"So what in the world brings you out here on a rainy Tuesday morning, Sherriff?" asked Mr. Kealoha to the very nervous and obviously distraught local HPD officer standing before him dripping in the downpour.

"Mr. Kealoha, you are one tough guy to get hold of. Don't you ever answer your phone?" officer Chong said, very uncomfortably shuffling his foot side to side in the puddle on the stone walkway leading to the edge of the lanai at the front of the ranch house.

"Mr. Kealoha, I have some terrible news. It's about Samuel .... He's missing on Kauai and an extensive search is underway .... Have you not heard this on TV?!" blurted out Sergeant Chong.

"What! .... Mother come out here! Why, what? Where is our son? Where is Samuel?" questioned Mr. Kealoha, trying to get a handle on the entire cascading information.

"He was involved in a very dramatic ocean rescue at Barking Sands. I am sorry to report that after being swept out and around the right point – he has not been spotted since. That was yesterday at sunset. I am so, so sorry. All possible methods are being employed by Fire Rescue in conjunction with the Coast Guard. Also, many locals have pitched in to help find your son as quickly as possible. According to many eye witness accounts, the waves were absolutely horrendous, sir." Once again, Sergeant Chong lowered his head and could barely hold back his own emotions from overflowing.

By this point in time, both Mr. and Mrs. Kealoha had completely lost their composures and wept unabashedly.

"Bring down that chopper from Waimea – we leave immediately!" Mr. Kealoha said forcefully to Sergeant Chong. He turned and went in to pack two light bags, grab some climbing gear, and to place a call to the one and only surviving grandmother. She was in an extreme care facility and the call was a mere formality, for she would not even know the subject of it a few minutes later.

It was a very somber flight to Kauai with one fast refueling on Oahu. They were in a hammered Hughes 500C helicopter that all of the ranches used on occasion to help with some strays or heavy lifting into the back sections of the valley to keep the water flumes in repair.

* * * * * * *

POLIHALE STATE PARK, NORTHWEST SHORELINE, ISLAND OF KAUAI

Mr. and Mrs. Kealoha arrived at the Na Pali Coast by noon on Tuesday. It appeared to them that they were the last to arrive. Many Zodiacs, fishing boats of all sizes, a Coast Guard cutter and the Fire Rescue brilliant orange Bell Jet Ranger helicopter all worked the coastline. Three other tour helicopters, searched non-stop, as well, at the expense of one Mr. Fujitani. Mr. Fujitani was still in great distress. He owed the young Mr. Kealoha, Samuel, his entire world's existence. After all, Samuel had saved his entire family and his very bloodline.

The pilot for *Mauna Mountain Helicopters* simply followed Mr. Kealoha's demands. He knew they were late, and he had been involved in too many search-and-rescues that had become, sadly, body recovery missions. From what he could see, unfortunately, this was one of them. He really liked the Kealoha family, and this was so very sad beyond belief.

Putting the chopper down at the last known location of Samuel, Mrs. Kealoha got out and was immediately shielded from the relentless media by

Samuel's friends, many who had dropped everything and arrived there by any means possible.

Nalu, William, Akina, Johnny had all arrived together by a 'borrowed' airplane out of Hilo. Makani and Jesse had gotten an early flight, a rent-a-wreck and had just gotten to this desolate far point about an hour earlier.

They tried to help Mrs. Kealoha get caught up on all of the events that transpired. The information was of no comfort. She did not care if the media was lauding her son as a hero having saved two families on the same day on two different islands. She did not care that they wished to talk about his brilliant skills or innate open ocean knowledge.

She only wanted him found – now! Unhurt and safe for her to hug, that's all. Nothing more, nothing less.

Surf was falling but was still very very large. People searched by land, sea, and air for any signs of any kind. Lots of debris was found, pushed in by the ocean sets and high tides, but it was all unrelated.

As soon as Mr. Kealoha saw the coastline, the waves and wicked currents that intertwined through the broken giant slivers of rock shards and shelves, he knew that if Samuel was to be found he'd of been found by now, especially with the tremendous outpouring of help and aloha by all involved. To their extreme credit, the local Barking Sands Missile Base Battalion Commander had even used the rescue as a 'military exercise' and put every able bodied person to the task.

All to no avail.

Then the Kealohas found out about all of the events that had occurred at the time of Samuel's disappearance, including the injury of Kulei who was recuperating at the local hospital with a shattered leg and a broken heart.

They also heard of the terrible crash that ensued when the Blazer, piloted by an overzealous driver, went off the road at an extreme rate of speed, cart wheeled into a barren section of rocks and threw out both occupants. Kimi, the blonde, was only slightly hurt with a mild concussion. She had zero recollection of events leading up to and including the horrific crash. Kimi would be fine and her parents were on their way from Iowa to retrieve her. It appeared she'd be missing the rest of her summer in Hawaii.

But, alas, Noe did not fare as well – not at all. She died on impact. Never moved according to the search and rescue EMS man. They diverted from Samuel's rescue when they caught a glimpse of the destroyed and still smoking Blazer in the pile of rocks that had two bodies nearby.

72

They picked up Kimi, covered Noe, and then swooped in and grabbed Kulei who had gone into deep shock by then. Heli-rescue did a quick pass down the Na Pali, saw no signs of Samuel, and straight-lined Kimi and Kulei as fast as possible to the landing pad at the hospital.

HPD, along with a land based fire rescue unit, recovered Noe's body. Everyone wept. Noe was well known as the impossibly pretty Kauai girl. She was that year's entry from Kauai for the *Miss Aloha Hawaii Pageant*. Everyone expected her to win. Her family was well liked, and Noe was loved. How sad - her parents and siblings could not be consoled.

After refueling twice more, dark closed in and all waited with a small fire burning at the pristine stretch of beach which had lost its luster for so many people, families and friends.

Three days later, the search was officially called off. Mr. and Mrs. Kealoha and many others looked for weeks to no avail – not a single shred of evidence was ever found concerning the final disposition of young Mr. Samuel Kealoha.

*   *   *   *   *   *   *

HAIWIKI RANCH, KOHALA MOUNTAINS, ISLAND OF HAWAII

Thirty days of morning had gone by and the Kealohas had sent invitations far and wide to all of the friends of Samuel and Noe, their families, and, of course, all of the people involved in the extensive search that had been performed. The only people not invited were the TV news crews and journalist that so documented, poked, probed and prodded all in the chase for ratings. Even though, in this particular instance, no elaborations of any kind were necessary.

Yet the "star crossed lovers" innuendo was way too much for both families and neither could stand to watch the news much anymore.

KNZO's news babe was the best at what she did and milked it evening after evening. Her final summation went like this:

"It has become apparent that the final chapter of the late Mr. Samuel Kealoha has come to light. Knowing, accurately of course, that young Mr. Kealoha had been involved in two dramatic ocean rescues, successfully I might say, of two entire families. First the dramatic boat accident here on Oahu on the late morning and early afternoon of a Monday last month. Including also the extreme heroic efforts to save the entire Fujitani family of Osaka, Japan at the most treacherous of locations at the far point of Barking Sands Beach, officially known as Polihale State Park. But this *Flash Traffic and Exclusive* new information has just been gleaned by reliable sources. Even earlier, that very same day – that very morning just after sunrise – young Mr. Samuel Kealoha effectuated the

73

rescue of an entire family along with the CPR life saving recovery of their mother vacationing on Maui at Baldwin Beach Park. It can now be said, and indeed should be shouted for all to hear, that young Mr. Kealoha shall go down in Hawaiian lore and legend as the true embodiment of "Ocean Hero Extraordinaire". He has gone from hero to legend and now, Samuel Kealoha, is of mythological status."

"And you have heard it first, here on KNZO news – Mealani Trask-Talbott reporting. More news at 10:00 p.m. this evening."

It was amazing who actually showed up at the potluck dinner and bonfire at the ranch for Samuel's memorial get-together – of course all of his friends showed up and even a few new ones. Four girls claimed that they had been the love of his life. None were. Even the Commander of the Barking Sands Missile Range made an appearance with six honor guards fully dressed in formal military attire. The party was well under way when slowly a black limousine wound its way up the very long driveway. Out of it came the entire Fujitani family, very sober and all dressed in formal black attire. Mr. Fujitani walked directly to Mr. Kealoha, and, with no words of any kind bowed before him, got on one knee, and presented Mr. Kealoha their family's last remaining Samurai sword. An exquisite museum quality piece from the days of the Shogun and Imperial Japan; it was an original and legendary *Masamune Super Blade* that carried the soul of the patriarch of the Fujitani clan.

They both wept.

Mrs. Fujitani presented Mrs. Kealoha with a hand carved box full of priceless *Mikimoto* black pearls, laced all into one braided six-foot long strand.

They wept as well.

Mr. Kealoha, always the best of hosts, walked the Fujitani children over to Paint the Pony who was streaching and leaning over the fence. He gave each of them one mountain apple to feed Paint. They instantly became enthralled with ranch living. Wide open space to Japanese nationals was as foreign as the moon to them and a feisty horse made it even better!

Mr. Fujitani and Mr. Kealoha continued a quiet walk along the pathway. When they got to the old cottage built by Mr. Tanaka-san [-term of fondness, respect], Mr. Fujitani got very excited and animated, pointing at the handicraft and woodwork, *soji doors*, *furo* [steaming bath] made from koa planks and one sheet of half-inch thick copper.

Then he saw the bells, went absolutely still and resolutely pointed at them in stunned disbelief. Then very formally bowed low to Mr. Kealoha once again. A few minutes later, they continued their circle back to the gathering crowd.

A raging bonfire burned as the day slowly melded into night. People talked, remembered and quietly cried. Just at sunset, a lone rider on a magnificent black Arabian, dressed in a formal holoku white Hawaiian dress and dripping with leis slowly came into the circle of light, as the fire blazed and the sun cast a myriad of colors from horizon to mountains above.

She got off and let the Arabian walk over to muzzle with Paint the Pony over the split railed fence.

Grace walked over, unwound the long maile strands into two separate leis and offered one to Mrs. Kealoha and the other to Mr. Kealoha. She simply said, "I am so sorry about Samuel. May AKUA ALMIGHTY [GOD ALMIGHTY] bless you, comfort you and hold you, even now, in this time of your terrible loss." Then the three of them hugged and cried and even laughed, just a touch, as they noticed how thrilled Paint was with the magnificent Arabian.

Later on, The Boys busted out some guitars and the girls did some spontaneous hulas. They all sang the songs they knew, whoever would and could remember the lyrics as songs drifted on the evenings' twilight.

As a lull enveloped the surroundings, and with Grace borrowing a well-used guitar, she started to play a haunting melody that slowly morphed into her rendition of *If* by *Bread*. She sang it with such sweet conviction that the air went still, time collapsed upon its self, and the moonrise cast a pale light of redemption on all of the souls congregated there. Then she sang it in Hawaiian, as down at the gazebo at The Point so long ago – at least one young lifetime ago – and a dry eye could not be found. Even the stoic Fujitani clan understood the magnitude of the occasion and wept openly for the first time in their lives.

Paint the Pony and the Arabian could have cared less. They nuzzled and became instantly the best of friends for life.

Mr. Kealoha with the Missus at his side, calmly made an announcement well into the evening, "Everyone is welcome, indeed expected, to be at Hapuna Beach tomorrow late afternoon. We are going to have a final paddle out, a celebration of life, and a final aloha for our only son Samuel. Please attend. We are going to bed now. Stay and enjoy the evening as long as you wish."

No one had noticed that the jet-black Arabian slowly descended the long driveway with Grace as the rider or the brilliance of the stars overhead that illuminated her way. Although, Paint the Pony noticed and walked alongside on the pasture side of the fence until he could walk no more.

* * * * * * *

HAPUNA BEACH STATE PARK, ISLAND OF HAWAII

It was a crystalline day, blue skies, zero clouds and unlimited visibility. Maui stood at stark relief to the northwest. Mauna Kea, *Mauna Loa*, Hualalai and the effervescent green hills of the Kohala Mountains oversaw the crowd gathered at Hapuna Beach for Samuel's memorial service on the water. Over two hundred various surfboards, sea kayaks, outriggers from one man to eight, small skiffs, along with fishing boats of all configurations, slowly gathered into the bay.

Earlier there had been an impromptu potluck luncheon in the large shelter that had people overflowing both into the lawn and the beach below. It was a day of mourning and celebration. Children's laughter helped lighten the burdens that remained.

Noe's parents and family joined the Kealohas in four outriggers that picked them up at the northern edge of the bay. At that point in time, the boats, surfboards and other vessels on the water gathered into a loose group of circles, one larger than the next so all could see. The crowd was estimated at over a thousand.

A Hawaiian Christian pastor from Haile Hill in Hilo took it all in, as he stood at the bow of a small skiff. He then chanted a greeting in Hawaiian.

This gave the crowd time to settle and grasp the reverence of the moment, the event and circumstances of the occasion.

The pastor, sensing the HOLY SPIRIT had indeed showed up, knew to keep it short and to the point.

He then began, "My fellow travelers on this beautiful Earth, look around, see that which ALMIGHTY GOD has created! What a marvelous world we inhabit, albeit for such a brief moment of time. For some among us, that time we are given to enjoy family, friends, brothers, sisters, neighbors and, even the sojourners whom walk amongst us, is oh too short."

"Samuel 'Pancho' Kealoha was one of those who had his time cut way too short. Many of us never even were afforded the opportunity to say goodbye. How unfortunate, how sad."

"Well, we are gathered today to say that final farewell. Goodbye, our dear son, friend, surfer, cowboy and, as it would be, mighty hero. You were an absolute example of all that is the highest qualities of the human spirit."

"Aloha, dear son, Samuel – aloha."

76

"It is written in the Holy Bible, the Living Word, and it proclaims in Ecclesiastes 7:

A good reputation is more valuable than costly perfume.

And the day you die is better than the day you are born.

Better to spend your time at funerals than at parties

After all, everyone dies –

so the living should take this to heart.

Sorrow is better than laughter,

for sadness has a refining influence on us.

A wise person thinks a lot about death,

while a fool thinks only about having a good time."

The pastor nodded at the Kealohas and Noe's parents. They all leaned over the rail and together reverently poured the ashes of Noe, along with some of the ashes scooped from the fire at the ranch they had the night before, into the crystal waters surrounding them.

The ashes slowly clouded the waters and plummeted toward the white sand bottom that shifted to and fro on the sea floor seventy feet below.

Everyone, in unison, softly sang the Hawaiian farewell song *Aloha Oi* while all that had gathered tossed lei after lei after lei at the ashes that were falling.

As the song tapered off, the pastor, as a means of formal dismissal, sang a solo of the *Hawaiian Doxology* … *"Ho'onani Ika Makua Mau"* [*Praise GOD from whom all blessings flow* …].

With the surface of the ocean covered in orchids, plumeria, ginger, lehua, tuber rose, maile and pikake, along with too many varieties of island bouquets to count, the crowd dispersed back to the beach and points beyond. From all the corners of the Earth, people had heard the story of one young hero. Who not knowing any other possible way, simply went, and in doing so, saved three entire families in the brief period of a single day without one single thought of hesitation or of his own safety.

They carried that story back with them to Australia and Fiji, Guam and Taiwan, Japan and Korea, Malaysia and Sumatra, New Zealand and California, Iowa and Kansas, Pennsylvania and Kentucky. One young couple sojourned from Brazil just to be part of something so much larger than themselves.

Even two tourists from Saskatchewan, having nothing better to do, took their cheap float mats, awkwardly paddled out and enjoyed the show. They were a little confused until the ashes dropped, but would talk about it for years to come as the highlight of their Hawaiian vacation.

Seems that tourists were everywhere – even at Samuel's funeral!

* * * * * * *

NA PALI COAST STATE PARK, NORTHWEST SHORELINE, ISLAND OF KAUAI

Although, a year later to the day of Samuel's Na Pali disappearance, a young hippie was hiking a far distant trail along Na Pali's rugged shore with his equally organic girlfriend. They found a single Churchill fin that was slightly tattered and softly broken in – that lone fin fit the hippie perfectly.

He bodysurfed all day with that single fin, caught the waves of his life – and lost it just at sunset, which forced him to come in. He ate a mango and mourned the loss. He never noticed the tiny little iridescent dragonfly snag a sliver of mango with the skin attached, then make off with it to the jungle waterfall behind their campsite. The dragonfly was blue with golden wings that rivaled the sun as they glistened in the falling light.

"Did you see that?" said his girlfriend, tanned all over with zero bikini lines.

"See what? " he asked not looking away from her.

"Never mind ... just a bit odd is all." They both laughed and spent the rest of the summer on the Na Pali coastline eating mangos and such other items as the fruits of love.

* * * * * * *

KAANAPALI BEACH, ISLAND OF MAUI

Divinely ordained as well, a year to the day that Samuel had ceased to walk the Earth and swim the seas, a perfectly preserved intricately woven pikake lei washed up upon the feet of a cute-as-could-be, now six-year-old, young lady with windswept and unruly curly hair. She had an attitude of fire to match her sparkling blue eyes as she played upon the sands of Kaanapali Beach in West Maui.

She reached down, noticed the blood red dragonfly that had been riding it darting towards Heaven. She scooped up the lei, put it around her neck then danced up the sand shouting, "Look Daddy – Samuel the Surfer sent this for me!"

Her father reached out, grabbed her hand, smiled and said, "That's nice Gracely – shall we get dinner?"

They walked hand in hand back to the far end of the golden sand beach as the sun set with a soft kindness to the west. Neither noticed the spectacular *green flash* [sunsets' last glimmer flashes brilliant green] or the dragonfly silhouetted momentarily in its glory.

10

One Glimpse

After Samuel's funeral and the dust had settled from so much in such a short period of time, summer came and went. The crew got ready for their try at college.

Nalu and Akina decided for Chaminade on Oahu. It was just like extending St. Joe's into grades thirteen thru sixteen, gradual changes for those two. They could handle nuns and the girls from Sacred Hearts High School were really pretty.

William couldn't be bothered any longer with college. It would cut into winter swells time, and besides, he really enjoyed tearing things apart, finding out what went wrong and then fixing them. Hopefully making them better in the process, and of course, with more power!

Johnny and Makani both joined Jesse at the local four-year branch campus of the University of Hawaii system – The University of Hawaii at Hilo – or 'Uhhhhhhhhh ...... ', as they liked to say.

Fall swept in with a change of swell direction. When the weather is perfect year round, one must notice the little things. With fall sweeping in, a new batch of collegians migrated to the fiftieth state from everywhere and for every possible reason, some good and proper, many not so much.

And that is when it started to get interesting both in Heaven and on Earth.

$$* \quad * \quad * \quad * \quad * \quad * \quad *$$

THE REALM

Noe leaned across the table and gently fed Samuel a tiny sliver of 'fish' dripping with shoyu and wasabi with a pair of simple bamboo chopsticks. She literally glowed; hair wavering in the breeze and her brown eyes dancing.

"What type of fish is this?" he said, after having the tenth piece delivered via the ultimate service.

"I'm not sure if it's even fish. It may be some type of funky fruit or something. I'm not even sure if we are carnivores any more. After all, I've been here longer than you, and if I don't know, you probably wouldn't either!" She laughed as she said it.

"You beat me here by what – two minutes or so?" he deadpanned, knowing that she was going to use that bit of information for eternity!

They had exchanged notes on their untimely demise with each other, both startled at how instant the transformation had been and how complete.

Samuel was grateful that the Japanese family had been rescued in their entirety – he wasn't sure. He'd lost track and was just saving whom he could.

Noe was still a little upset that she'd been driving, but was grateful that she had not taken anyone with her. She'd really liked Kimi, even if she was from Iowa and all.

"What is that sound – it drifts on and off of the wind?" Samuel turned his head, catching it once again on the cool breeze.

"Singing – new songs." Noe answered, knowingly with a twinkle in her eyes. One of her gifts back on Earth was the gift of song and that gift had not left her. So she quietly, and with elegant poise, chose to join in with what she heard on the wind, a song gently cascading along the River Of Life ……

The New Song

Oh oh oh – LORD I do pray

A simple jar of clay

On my knees I do pray

Please show me the way

Oh oh oh I say

LORD I need some joy today

Please show me the way

Oh oh oh ..... hallelujah

Oh oh oh ... oh oh oh

Oh oh oh ... oh oh oh

This simple jar of clay

A touch of Heaven divine

A simple song in time

One hug from the VINE

Please heal this broken jar of clay

Oh oh oh my LORD

Sing me a Heavenly chord

Of comfort and of joy

Find this lonely jar of clay

Hey hey hey hey hey

Bring me home to Heaven

Fix the scars within my eyes

Lead me home to the prize

Cleanse this broken jar of clay

*Oh L*ORD *I do pray*

Bring me home to Heaven...

Instantly, upon Noe finishing *The New Song*, they both found themselves walking along a dramatic stretch of lawn with trees all in rows. Blooms and fragrances overwhelmed them as they slowly walked toward a standing *Pillar of Light* [divine presence of GOD] in the not too far distance.

Somewhere along the way they started holding hands. Then they let go and started running to the Light – for they could wait no longer!

*   *   *   *   *   *   *

HAIWIKI RANCH, KOHALA MOUNTAINS, ISLAND OF HAWAII

On an Earthly slice of Heaven with green rolling fields of ultra-soft nerf grass and lone trees dotted about in awkward and impossible angles for shade, Paint the Pony frolicked, leaped and played in the wide open fields of the paddock opposite the lanai of the ranch house.

"That lolo horse has been at that for over an hour," Mr. Kealoha stated with a total lack of enthusiasm.

"Don't you mean loco? Shouldn't you stay true to your Mexican roots, dear?" offered the Missus with a subtle smile while handing him a cup of coffee which they'd found at an obscure shop, way down south, in Kau near Punalu'u.

"No matter how you say it, I think that Paint is just plain crazy today! And, have you noticed, it must be like some horse rain-dance or something, every time he runs like the wind with such wild abandon, it rains for days afterwards." He sipped his newfound favorite coffee.

"Hadn't noticed the correlation, Father. A horse rain-dance, now isn't that special!"

No one got too excited, except some of the critters up on the mountain on a typical evening.

By the third day of endless rain, everyone was over it, even the critters. Paint the Pony was in a stall. Literally both in the physical and by attitude, chomping at the hay bale that Mr. Kealoha had given him earlier. Katt the stray, that had just shown up on a rainy day, like Dogg had, stalked the *Pueo* high above in the rafters. The worst thing that could happen to Katt was if he actually got to it! That owl would shred him and eat him just like it did with everything else with which it came in contact. Dogg barely knew if he was alive, inside or outside of the barn. He'd shown up at the ranch looking rather old and worn already – that was ten years ago. Dogg hadn't done much since, except to bark at the occasional mongoose as it tried to pick off a chicken now and then. Judging from the piles of feathers here and there he must not have been very good at even that mundane guard duty.

Melancholy had crept into the ranch as a huge Pacific wide weather system dumped upon the entire eastern part of the state which included all of the Big Island, soaking everything from Kau to Kohala at all possible elevations.

It was late November and the new normal had settled into the Haiwiki Ranch owners and critters alike.

"Gonna have snow on the mountains after this gets *pau* [finished]," stated Father with a touch of weariness.

"We'll see – sometimes it's not for another month." Then the Missus re-thought her timeline, "Guess it is November."

This time it was a white limousine that slowly wound its way up the long driveway and deposited its passengers, once again, to the Kealohas' gentle doorstep late in the afternoon.

Rain kept falling relentlessly as Mr. Fujitani and two others leaped out and hustled to the lanai's safety zone.

Mr. Fujitani looked up, smiled, and bowed – and with a previously never seen much lighter heart – said, "Mr. Kealoha-san, good evening!"

Mr. Kealoha simply stuck out his hand and shook Mr. Fujitani's hand with great vigor, then offered, "Good to see you again. Aloha and sit down for a while. Have some coffee – it's that time of day."

Mr. Fujitani had hit the total limit of the English he'd learned and had his translator finish the remaining conversation. The three of them had come from their Gulf Stream II sitting down at the Keahole Airport just outside of Kona.

After a very long-winded batch of Japanese pleasantries, the translator got to the actual point of the visit. "Mr. Fujitani-san wishes for his expert to examine the bells he saw on the old Japanese cottage up there. Would you mind? If you were so kind to do so, Mr.Fujitani-san would be very appreciative. Although there is no way to ever repay the debts and already incurred kindnesses that are owed to your family."

"Why not now? Seems like it's letting up," Mr. K. answered while new waves and sheets of rain unloaded as he headed toward the cottage with blistering rain exploding all around.

They all dutifully followed; although none of them got the American humor, lost in translation and all.

They stood under the overhang and Mr. Fujitani's 'sidekick' looked at the bells, jaw hanging down and magnifying glass raised, sweeping side to side. The expert looked at Mr. Fujitani's translator and spoke a few sentences in brisk Japanese. The translator looked at Mr. Kealoha and asked, "Do these bells always ring, like this, when it rains? They appear to be almost singing, like they have a melody about them. Is that normal for these bells?"

Mr. K. nodded, a man of few words at various times. Trying to mentally figure out what these 'darned foreigners' were up to, a slightly mystified look showed across his face.

After some time, and with much Japanese-to-Japanese conversation, Mr. Fujitani (via translator) asked, "May we take them to our laboratory in Osaka to examine them? We are very intrigued by them, and I've followed in my father's footsteps researching items of Asian art and antiquities. We will treat them with the utmost care and return them fully intact."

He bowed; they all bowed.

After a deep thought, Mr. K. answered, "Only if, when you bring them back here, you bring your wife and children, along with a translator, for a family BBQ 'Paniolo Style'. That would give us all something to look forward to, Mr. Fujitani-san."

As the translator told Mr. K's answer to Mr. Fujitani, a huge smile broke out across his face. The expert was beside himself with unabashed joy, and the translator passed back to Mr. K., across the forever divide of broken languages, a deep heartfelt thank you.

The expert packaged the bells with extraordinary care in a crate made of sugi pine and filled with wood shavings. Packing the bells firmly in the middle, he cranked the lid down with long brass bolts. Obviously he'd come prepared for a favorable outcome.

With their treasure secured, they headed down the long driveway. Back to the exact opposite of Haiwiki Ranch's mountain location, to a city that knew only noise, hustle and endless work, Osaka, and all that it conveyed.

On the way back to their waiting private jet at Keahole airport Mr. Fujitani could not quit smiling. His expert affiliate with the vast knowledge, openly wept with joy - one single tear.

After all, he was Japanese.

11

Adjustments

Johnny was quietly sitting under the half-acre banyan tree growing in mid-campus at U.H. at Hilo, watching the girls walk down past him, going from the classrooms mauka to the 'temporary' trailer classrooms *makai* [towards the sea]. He noticed that everything needed painting. Well everything needed the mold and moss scrapped off, and then treated, and then painted.

He was waiting for 'Windy' and Jesse. They had a field trip planned for surfing the southeast coast, and he couldn't wait. He had signed up for the early bird schedule and those classes started at 6:30 a.m., allowing him to be done with his day at 11:00 a.m. – great schedule – if you went to bed at 9:00 p.m. the night before.

"Hey Nebraskaaaaaa, you ready?" digging a little at Jesse's obvious dislike for his northern neighbor.

"Kansas, Johnny, Kansas! What part of Kansas do we not understand?" They shook hands and half 'man-hugged' then wrestled a bit with some *Tai Kwon Do* [martial art] moves thrown about.

Then 'Windy' showed up, and while he talked, both Jesse and Johnny picked up their stuff and headed to the parking lot.

* * * * * * *

VILLAGE OF PAHOA, DISTRICT OF PUNA, ISLAND OF HAWAII

They stopped in Pahoa Town for Spam musubi and fuel. Johnny looked at his musubi, then at 'Windy' and said, "You know Pancho loved these things..."

First time 'Windy' was left speechless. They just looked at each other then at the crushed blue rock under their feet. It was too nice of a day to go 'there', so they didn't after a bit of silently sad silence.

"Spoke with Stan this morning at his surf shop – needed some wax. He said that Drain Pipes was smoking!" Johnny informed them.

"I'm not surfing there, guys, I'm still healing from the last time." Jesse was dead serious.

"You can hang on the beach with the other girls and watch the tourist burn their feet on the steaming black sand while we tear it apart," said Johnny, "Jesse are you still a 'tourist', being from Kansas and all?"

"Compromise, *Kalapana Beach*, Left Point?" Jesse offered.

"Left Point sounds good, but how about Pohoiki Second Bay. Oughta be awesome!"

Windy started in on a point-by-point comparison that went on and on and on and on. Finally, Windy was cut off by Jesse, by veering left at the intersection taking them towards Lava Tree State Park. The trusty green Rabbit, a VW four cylinder, four wheel independent suspension, four speed, wonder weapon, that held four people along with four short boards inside the car and was able to 'fly', took them rapidly towards the surf at Pohoiki.

Jesse's driving was not for the faint of heart. It was one of the many reasons he was at college in Hawaii – trying to keep him from losing his license permanently. According to the last judge that he'd been in front of, Jesse had officially been given his 'last' second chance at redemption.

* * * * * * *

TOWN OF ATWOOD, KANSAS

His senior year of high school he'd borrowed his brother's '72 Corvette Stingray on a Friday night after the football game. On his way to the 'kegger' with his 'babe of the moment' he blew through radar at a little over 135 mph and didn't even know it. When he saw the lights in his rearview mirror – a fair distance down the road – he accelerated and lost them, just in case they were for

88

him. Then he outran a second cop but was eventually stopped at the border into Nebraska, by then he was cruising at the speed limit. Nebraska's finest escorted him back to their Kansas compatriots – giving him to their southern neighbors since they didn't have any problem with the youngster that showed up on their state line driving at a mere 65 mph.

The first cop he had outrun was livid and held nothing back at the hearing in front of the judge. He'd been disrespected, lost in the dust, and it angered him greatly. The second Kansas State Trooper was a little more philosophical and had considerably more humor – since he'd been in a Cessna Airplane – and it was the first time he'd ever been left in the dust by any terrestrial vehicle!

The honorable judge took it all in, gave Jesse a one year's suspension, a stern warning and a livid lecture that nearly melted his eyes and ears on the importance of growing up and achieving some level of responsibility.

It did not help that the girl with him that night was the judge's niece.

It was Jesse's senior year in high school, his 'girlfriend' wanted more 'commitment' than he was at all ready to provide. What was even weirder was that her 'friends' wanted him 'commitment' or not. What is it with these chics?

On a fluke, and while doing some actual research that cross blended colleges with applicable driver license application restrictions, Jesse had discovered that Hawaii, as far as driver license applications went, did not have reciprocity with Kansas, and that they also had a four year branch campus in Hilo that he could easily get into. Two for one! Nice.

And, just maybe, the girls were not so demanding or devious, just maybe.

* * * * * * *

ISAAC HALE BEACH PARK, DISTRICT OF PUNA, ISLAND OF HAWAII

Jesse made the next right at the 'Y', going into the chicanes and the rolling portion of the Pohoiki Road, down through the mango trees tunnel and final four wheel drift into the parking area. Johnny and 'Windy' both trembled 'til the very moment the VW Rabbit came to a complete rest, overlooking Pohoiki Bay.

Together they got out, looked over the built up wall of lava rubble, and together, in awe, they simply voiced, "Perfect!"

* * * * * * *

WAIKIKI, ISLAND OF OAHU

Two hundred some odd miles to the west-northwest their big city cohorts, Akina and Nalu were adjusting to three things, really, maybe four. College life in general – Chaminade really was an extension of St. Joe – but with a whole lot more freedom. Nobody cared how 'they'd' done it back in Hilo. They'd both gotten new jobs. Auntie Hula's's wasn't on Oahu, so of course they became Pedi Cab Drivers in Waikiki. It was wickedly fun, really hard work, which kept them in shape, and it paid amazingly well. One thing they had learned at Auntie Hula's was to entertain the customers and that helped immensely with the tips – thank you Auntie Hula's!

New school, new job, new town – Waikiki city living was the most difficult to overcome, minimal family support made it very hard to adjust. Both in the frustrations of getting around, but also in the cold emotional aspects of grinding against people they didn't know or understand, and in many instances, they outright loathed.

But the fourth item of adjustment helped them to overlook any other negative factors – girls! Lots of them, many outrageously pretty. 'Wow' hardly even began to cover the depth of the volume of sweethearts that encircled them on a daily basis.

Cruising through Waikiki on a late fall evening, in a torn to shreds eight year old Camaro beach car, windows down with *C&K* playing on the radio their latest hit, Nalu said, "Look at that one! Might be the most awesome girl I've ever seen!"

Akina wholeheartedly agreed, "I'm telling you – prettiest girl on Earth – nice blue dress, makes her look fabulous!"

Nalu, "What blue dress? She's in a red sarong!"

The two new Oahu boys cross glanced and realized that the prettiest girl on Earth was actually a Filipino chick in a red silk sarong on Akina's side of the Camaro and a blonde haired sweetheart in a blue sundress on Nalu's.

Only on Oahu in the late seventies could this mix even be possible in all of America. Nalu and Akina were both correct. Both lovely ladies could easily lay claim to the prettiest girl on Earth. They hooted, the girls waved and smiled – the evening progressed - typical Waikiki.

"I hear the glider-port up on the north shore is really cool, kinda want to do that," Nalu made conversation.

"Like hang gliding with the delta wing – you know like Superman style?" asked Akina.

"No, the ones that have the long wings and enclosed canopies – look like planes without engines" answered Nalu.

"No engines ... seems like a waste." Akina changed the subject, "It's our turn to get the beer and set up; it is full moon – OWOOOOO!!!"

* * * * * * *

DIAMOND HEAD, ISLAND OF OAHU

It was the monthly Howling Full Moon Party for *The Boys* and their few chosen buddies. They'd started it a few months earlier, four of them and a few friends from UH Manoa and Hawaii Pacific University. The idea came to them while drinking beer on the roof and howling at the full moon over the surf break at the base of the crater. So they each invited ten hot chicks and no other guys. It was awesome for the ten guys but not so much for the hundred plus girls as they slowly realized, as the evening wore on, that there would be no other boys arriving.

"The Boys Club" had a high attrition rate of girls not coming to the next party, but some did, and it seemed that – on Oahu – the list of pretty girls was bordering infinity.

Somehow they had fallen into renting an old dilapidated house in the world's most expensive subdivision – Diamond Head. The views were outrageous, the surf could be epic at times – although mostly blown out – and the neighbors were fairly docile.

Except for one – who happened to be a lowly District Judge - who turned them in every month at exactly 10:00 p.m. for a disturbing the peace violation; it was codified law and he was real big on that type of technocratic detail.

They paid the fifty-dollar fine, then went on and partied 'til 2:00 a.m. figuring that 'The Judge' was constipated and had never had a single day of fun in his entire life.

'The Judge', whom was at times constipated, and was always not having any fun, just couldn't take the racket. After all, he was 'important' and had things to do, as long as it didn't involve church, on a Sunday morning.

The young cops on night patrol that issued the tickets would circle back after their shifts to hang out because they'd never seen so many great looking babes in one spot. In exchange they'd write fictitious names on the tickets for *The Boys* so no one really got into any lingering troubles with their constipated unhappy neighbor.

Between the encounter with Grace, the tragic events with Samuel, and the realization that college was grades thirteen thru sixteen, Nalu and Akina, along with most of the others, would occasionally consider their circumstances. The conversation would shift to religion and the spiritual at the strangest times –

surfing during the long lulls between sets, or when they were really hung over on a Sunday morning – but mostly when they thought about where would Samuel or Timmy be now? What would they be doing? Was there a Heaven and GOD? The nuns sure beat that in to them time after time at the burning end of a yardstick swung with deadly accuracy! And if this was the prime of life and they were having so much 'fun', all things considered, there had to be more to life. Where were the nice girls? They hadn't met them yet, and they'd partied with hundreds by this point in time!

A weird melancholy of 'fun' settled in on them, and they could not quite put their finger on the solution. They'd defer the answer knowing they had at least four years of confusion to find a way to the other side of the equation – but only if they lived!

They had four years and probably at least another forty "disturbing the peace" citations to pay. Maybe the light would shine upon them too.

12

Unknown Origin

Slightly less than 4,000 miles to the west-west-northwest from Hawaii Nei, in the city of Osaka, Mr. Fujitani quietly left *Osaka Natural Gas Company's* headquarters and headed to a non-descript warehouse section of the industrial cityscape. He headed to a huge building, four stories tall and bland as could be. That building was at the end of a gritty street. His driver waved at the security guards, whom promptly bowed and opened the electric gate to receive them.

Only a handful of people in Japan understood the dynamics of how the business society really worked. Mr. Fujitani was one of them that very much understood the methods of structure and who and what ran his country. Osaka Natural Gas Company, [aka ONGCO] including its wholly owned subsidiaries and their related companies, was part of a seventeen corporation 'Super Group' or Keiretsu, a loosely knit together group of unrelated industries that chose to work with each other as a means to ensure their mutual viability for generations to come.

America's long term planning was measured in years. For the Japanese, long term planning was measured in centuries.

Mr. Fujitani's family enterprises had generated millions of dollars in profits per month, and all was measured in dollars, since the end of WWII. This allowed him lots of flexibility, and he could work on projects both known and unknown with tremendous resources being brought to bear.

With the extremely powerful and ultra-connected Keiretsu, which he'd been made a board member of recently, Mr. Fujitani had, for the era, virtually free range, trajectory and methods at his complete disposal.

He hung his Armani jacket up and pulled down a white smock, went through two more checkpoints, one by voice and one by pass code, then entered into a world class laboratory clean room with all of the latest computing, measuring, analysis, chemistry, micro and macro visual examination and physical testing equipment known to man. Much of the technology surrounding him was not available to the general population or industry. Much of it governments didn't even possess or even know about, and if they did, not all of them could afford to own them.

His Keiretsu involved air and space design, advanced car manufacturing, global trade, chemical engineering, international banking, design applications, radiometric reading, electric and natural gas power generation and much much more. Together they controlled over 15% of Japan's entire economy. Few knew of their Keiretsu, even fewer knew the influence they wielded across *Nippon* [Japan] and increasingly all of Asia.

What they couldn't take and keep in the war, they had determined to simply purchase as and when possible.

"What have we discovered, Anji-san?" Mr.Fujitani asked the lead project manager of the working group assigned to oversee 'The Singing Bells' matter.

"Oh, Mr. Fujitani-san – pleasure to see you in such good health! Hawaii was fortuitous to you Mr. Fujitani-san," Anji-san said with a very deep bow and massive formality.

He continued, "The 'bells' are highly unusual, beyond anything I'd ever expected. At this point in time we have not only been unable to determine their date of manufacture, but we cannot even determine the type of materials used to create them. Which adds even one more question to the deep mystery you've presented before me. Whom, or what, would possibly have the skills and advanced technological manufacturing processes to create such magnificent treasure?"

"At this stage they are an enigma." He was very bewildered, and it showed as he lowered his head and looked like he'd gotten very little rest.

"Or what? Not who – you said 'or what'. What for ever do you mean, Mr. Anji-san?" asked Mr. Fujitani, now staring with a stunned expression at the bells hanging before them.

94

They hung from stainless steel laboratory latticework with a hole above and a small tank below.

"We do have one advancement in knowledge, I shall demonstrate. They will only 'sing' with the purest of pure spring or rainwater. No other type of water will release their native tones. This is pure Himalayan glacial ice, flown in and melted just for this demonstration – behold," and he opened a ball valve allowing the water to cascade from the hole above – over the bells – and into the tank below.

The bells 'sang' a glorious tune. Mr. Anji-san played with the volume of water changing the flow rates and simultaneously changing the tonal qualities of the bells as the water increased and decreased.

"It is so fortunate that the location of your discovery was in such a pristine environment. My research indicates that with the prevailing weather patterns your bells enjoyed some of the cleanest rainfall possible in this industrial age. Our rainwater here in Osaka Prefecture will not release their song, and that, my dear friend, is a hard thing to discover. Bad for our beloved Nippon. We must do better in our manufacturing sectors. Yet that, Mr. Fujitani-san, is a different matter."

"One more item of extreme interest. There appears to be markings under the patina of unknown origin. I'm assembling a team to help me fathom the depths of that aspect, along with the other quandaries as well. One gentle lady is from here – your Soni [nobel communicator] with her language skills will be assisting. She'll make herself available as soon as the other two get here."

"Who are the other two? Where are you bringing them in from?" asked Mr. Fujitani.

"Both are Americans. One is from Carnegie Mellon University in Pittsburgh; the other is from Boston's Massachusetts Institute of Technology. I can't remember their names. I just call the one Dr. *MIT* and the other Dr. *CMU*. Gaijin – all the same, can't tell any of them apart – they all look alike to me!"

They both looked at each other and had an uncontrolled belly laugh - first time for each of them in some time – and then they quietly and with great reverence stared at the bells hanging before them that were still singing in that strange harmonic melody from ages past.

13

Adventures

Really dense deep rich fog was trying to burn off of the top of the ranch as the morning light shined from above, putting the force of Heaven upon it. The weight was immense, but the progress was slow.

Mr. Kealoha finished a cup of Kau coffee and adjusted the handmade, workbelt-saddle he had custom built for Paint. The horse needed to earn his living; this was a working ranch after all. Paint stood quietly – unfazed by the morning's coming light duty chores ahead.

They had gotten into a routine of walking one paddock a week – usually just before placing the cattle into it to lower the ever growing pasture. Rain, sun, rain, sun, rain, sun – the grass grew so fast it almost kept Mr. and Mrs. Kealoha awake at night!

Dogg was doing an excellent impression of a welcome mat lying at the entrance of the barn. Katt was in the rafters with one paw dangling – oblivious to everything around. Gertrude the chicken was the only productive member in the critter kingdom. She and her fellow hens laid about five eggs total per day – since they were free range. It was always a mystery if all eggs were actually found or not. Nasty Kyle, the wicked little Banty Rooster, had just showed up one day. He was probably an escapee from a local Filipino cockfight. He was always aggressive, obnoxious and just plain mean. It was spooked at every little thing; Nasty Klye was mad about his unplanned forced exile and ready to do battle in a heartbeat, and if he hadn't been excellent at keeping Gertrude and the other chickens in order and happy. If he didn't eat his weight in insects daily, keeping the poisonous centipedes in check, he'd have been blasted to a dusting of feathers long ago.

Mr. Kealoha gave Mother a peck on the cheek, told her he and Paint were going to work Number 5 Paddock and ought to be back by lunchtime and that pie would be nice. She looked up from her coffee and quilting, smiled – a smile that spoke all that needed to be said.

Paint walked dutifully beside Mr. Kealoha as they worked the wire on the fencing as the fog melted away to the day that was forming above them. The grass was three feet thick in places and spongy – making the four mile walk quite the trek. Paint's job was easy. He grazed and was the 'horse tool belt', Mr. Kealoha's job was as hard as he wished to make it. Today was relatively easy work – no smash downs from the tree line of robusta eucalyptus – just a few minor repairs so far. Broken wire here – pulled staple there – all to be expected and easy enough to fix.

At about halfway into the circuit, and at the highest point, a lone pueo sat on a fence post. It turned its head and twisted it ninety degrees clockwise then one hundred eighty degrees back counter clockwise to apprise its invaders that dared to wonder into its domain. Hawaiian owls don't tolerate interlopers well, but seeing the size of the invading forces, it lifted off and melted into the mist as ghost to white.

"What in the world was this thing eating?" asked Mr. Kealoha to Paint, not expecting much in the way of a reply. Paint actually snorted and somewhat startled him with his return on the comment.

Upon inspection, it was obvious that the Pueo was feasting on an *Alala* – the rarest bird on Earth and virtually extinct – the Hawaiian crow. What a stupid bird, couldn't out fly a night bird! No wonder they were so rare and endangered!

They picked up the pace as the morning wore on and the walk turned downhill. Mr. K., being a rancher, knew that when you can step on the head of your shadow it's time for lunch.

About half mile out, Paint got really excited. First snorting, then up on his back legs and into the air pawing – then front - then circles with more snorts. Paint took off at a dead gallop towards the ranch house. Mr. Kealoha couldn't believe it when he saw that horse clear the gate separating the paddocks on a dead run. Now ain't that something he thought! Must be some excitement down below. He picked up his pace just by a bit – after all he didn't see any smoke and hadn't heard any gunfire.

Sitting on the porch with Mother was Grace, her Arabian stood against the fence nuzzling with Paint. Love had returned to the stables of Haiwiki Ranch!

"Nice to see you Grace; actually wonderful! We don't get visitors as often as we'd like!" He may have said it with a little too much exuberance for the Missus' sake; it was hard for any man not to notice how elegantly beautiful Grace was - even in blue jeans and cowboy boots – maybe especially in blue jeans and cowboy boots!

The Missus gave Father 'the look'; he got it. Everyone settled in to small talk and light lunch together. Mrs. Kealoha hadn't made pie, but she did make guava cake, and it was wonderful.

After lunch, Grace got to the question she'd come to ask, "I'm going sailing and it will be a rather involved and extended journey. Could I board my Arabian with your Paint? They get along magnificently, and I hoped you could afford me some help with this problem I have to resolve rather soon, even today?" She smiled and held the cup of coffee on her lap. "I'll leave money for her food and upkeep – and a little extra should she have any special needs; one never knows the expenses of a horse after all."

Everyone looked at Paint leaning as far as possible over the fence rail! The Missus nodded. It was settled – Paint had a friend, the Arabian had temporary housing and Grace had a problem solved.

As she passed the envelope stuffed full of twenties to Mrs. Kealoha, she said, "What an absolutely lovely American Tobiano Paint. He's even got the booties and star on his forehead – marvelous!" Then with a twinkle in her eyes, "Maybe a foal in the fall would be compensation for your troubles. I've never seen an Arabian-Paint mix, not in Hawaii Nei – wouldn't that be something!" She was almost giddy.

Grace, with many alohas and hugs, went on down the driveway and off on her adventure. As she drove down the long, long driveway, Mr. Kealoha looked at the glorious wife of his tucked under his arm and stated, "She's smart and observant enough to know he's a Tobiano Paint - a true American Paint – but she doesn't notice that Paint is a gelding, that's just plain *pupule* [stupid] if you ask me."

The Missus wacked him with her apron she had over her shoulder and said, "Who knows? Maybe she knows something we don't? Miracles upon occasion do happen, and these two having a foal – now that would be a miracle!"

He walked over, opened the gate, and the Arabian pranced into a slice of green shimmering pasture like a jewel from far away. Then, immediately galloped out of sight with Paint the Pony racing after her to his heart's content.

* * * * * * *

CITY OF HILO, ISLAND OF HAWAII

Two days later, at the crack of dawn, Mauna Kea and Mauna Loa glowed pink-pale-purple tinting their summits that were cast in pure white snowcaps. Hilo Town shook the willing and unwilling awake for the day's journey of dawn. Tidal pools stood dead calm with schools of *manini* [tiny fish] darting about. Ravenous little baby hammerhead sharks worked the inside of the bay for an early snack. Teachers prepped for students; students slowly were prodded towards their day of pretending to learn. While the sugar cane companies changed shifts, fired up various diesel engines on tracked loaders, crawlers, haulers – watching their black-brown, first plumes of exhaust, briefly pollute the cleanest air on Earth. The fleet of crop dusters woke up to terrorize the cane fields up and down the Hamakua coastline – spraying fertilizer, time released *Ozmocote*, to boost the cane's growth rates. Ultimately paying for their flight time, cost and efforts by considerably higher yields of more tons per acre of sugarcane harvested.

Technocrats shuffled to the various office buildings since Hilo was the county seat of government, performing functions no one wanted. Functions that any civil society demanded be done, but all loved to hate regardless.

Breakfasts of fried rice to breaded Spam, from traditional All American Fruit Loops to a lone mango being eaten while looking for the perfect fishing spot for the day down by King's Landing. *Loco Mocos* at *Café 1000* were being cooked and sold by the dozens, *malasadas* [donut holes] out the back by the tens of dozens, boxes full of them for the 10:00 a.m. coffee break that was never missed.

It was a morning as usual in Hilo Town, but a lone 69-foot, double steel hauled, twin mast schooner silently left the harbor for points unknown. A lone figure was at the helm. Her hair was glory in the wind, and the smile on her face helped to light the coming dawn.

Grace was at the helm; the most natural place for her to be. She was on a *Voyage Of Discovery* – helping to plan the long-term vision of her friends, a new generation of the ancient Polynesian navigators. Discovering anew; since before time was counted, numbered, stamped, correlated and maps existed. She was going to help re-create the great southern passages as a way to expand the grasp of her friends at the *Polynesian Voyaging Society* and their beloved newly constructed, yet of of ancient design, *Ho'okulea* open ocean voyaging canoe.

Her dreams coincided with some of theirs, and today at this very hour in a well-stocked sturdy blue water vessel, her journey would begin. Her voyage into the great Southern Ocean was the endless journey of adventure and her yacht was simply called: *THE FAITH*

14

Fragments Of Truths

Gritty and various shades of unkempt were all that showed on the streets surrounding an ever increasing excitement in the ultra high tech labs of the pristine clean rooms at the Keiretsu Laboratory Complex. Great strides were being pressed upon the enigma at hand.

How were these bells, seemingly so insignificant, manufactured? Created would be a better term – and an even more important truth, by whom?

"Mr. Fujitani-san, time to make your way here. Sorry for such a call at such an hour. Sorry to disturb you, sir, but we have begun to get preliminary bits of information. Fragments of truths. Please come at your earliest convenience, sir," said the project manager Mr. Anji, having awoken Mr. Fujitani at 3:33 a.m. on a Sunday morning.

There was no use trying to go back to sleep after such news – he couldn't have if he wanted to. He was the most thrilled of anyone. Knowing the bells unique nature, he was on his way with his very sleepy driver in less than twenty minutes.

After completing the security that never slept, Mr. Fujitani was greeted by the entire team without any of the usual formalities. Taking him into a central boardroom, they started immediately with just a few of the findings, giving him various points in a disconnected format.

Coffee had been everyone's best friend for the past ninety-six hours.

Dr. CMU, holding doctorates in material sciences, applied technologies along with various other disciplines, spoke directly to Mr. Fujitani in excited tones. Soni - the young, twenty-something secretary with her own doctorate in advanced linguistics along with ancient alphabets and origins, antiquities studies and verifications of Asian artifacts – interpreted for Dr. CMU.

He continued, "High resolution and high definition slides – now projected before you shall help us shed some light on the materials used, manufacturers' methodologies and techniques to achieve such results as these bells present before us. First, please note the total and complex patina of all surfaces of these bells." He showed slide after slide in color, revealing a deep and complete coating upon the bells in glorious hews and shades, "Also please note the curvilinear shapes of the bells themselves, a rounded rectangular box design with falling away corners and slightly concave tops."

"We, as a team, have used various devices to try and get a handle on these bells, but by using two items not currently available in any other lab that I've been in, advanced optical microscopy, and the latest in XRF Elemental Analysis we have found three startling realities.

"The outer 'bell' appears to have been created by the hollowing of an extremely large and flawless matrix clear diamond. If that is indeed the case – these twelve bells used the twelve largest flawless diamonds to have ever been found on Earth."

Every person in the room was of rapt attention.

"Second," he continued on, "what we thought was an enamel band of decorative paint at the base perimeter of each bell – this deep blue/black line at the bottom, " he used a pointer to show his colleagues the deep blue line at the bottom of each on the slide that was now being projected before them, "that line of 'enamel paint' upon microscopic inspection is actually one piece of finely cut sapphire of the purest quality. Current day Burma is the only spot on Earth that we know of to have such clear flawless quality sapphire with this particular color. Once again, the sapphires these twelve bells needed for this application, would have involved the twelve largest sapphires - of flawless quality - to have ever been mined on Earth and then to be used in this manufacture."

It was now 4:35 a.m., and Mr. Fujitani hadn't been this excited since his father had brought his future wife home for his review and approval. Many Keiretsu marriages were still very much arranged – quietly of course.

"Now the third item of interest. The inner bell, if you will, is of the purest gold. This we could test with the tiniest of samples. It is from, of all places, Peru, South America. How, why, when? Please do not ask me any of those questions. But the diamonds almost had to have come from either South Africa or Zaire, the sapphire from Burma and the gold from South America!"

"Who are these people?!" Dr. CMU sat down abruptly, even more at a losss than when he started.

It immediately became Dr. MIT's turn, he did not hesitate or slow the process. He was a world class scientist in his own right, but his real expertise that was rivaled by very few others on Earth were optics and sound. Both theoretical and practical applications thereof.

Dr. MIT started, "Please note the complex tonal qualities generated by these 'bells'. 'Bells' does not do them justice. Each of these instruments is separately tuned one octave apart, all appear to have a limitless range. Played by the running of pure water – together they sing. Giving off a depth of sounds at various flow rates that could rival any orchestra ever assembled by man!" He smiled unabashedly – being in tweed and looking beyond frumpy – it made everyone smile also. Having lightened the mood, as he often did in his classrooms in Boston, he carried on. "Their range goes well past the audible hearing spectrum of 20,000 Hz for humans, and before we installed the new sound deadening devices, we annoyed and awakened every dog in Osaka. It appears that the akita were especially angry about our findings. We also found that by projecting sounds at the 'bells' themselves they resonated back a matching tone. How odd that was! Just a side note, it has been well documented that advance sound waves of an approaching earthquake creates the same anxiousness in certain animals. It appears that one function of these bells may have been a well-advanced earthquake early warning system for humans. That is uncertain at this time."

"Those findings are neither here nor there – the exciting part is the sound findings coupled with the optical findings – put the two together and …. "

He then walked the group over to the bells themselves, turned on the water flow, and threw a switch on the wall beside him that produced true natural daylight from a specialty fixture, amplified, it shown directly from below on the bells sapphire rings. Twelve bells, from a far away ranch in the Kohala Mountains located on the furthest archipelago in the wildest ocean on Earth, shown like stars and cast well defined patterns on the walls. Creating gasps of awe from the souls gathered round.

Patterns, not of random sequence, but of an obvious and highly delicate type of writing, being of unknown origins, shown all about them.

Then, Dr. MIT upped the ante. He changed the water flow rates and the intensity of the white light beam – and with that - each side of each bell, north south, east, west – lit up separately. Each face told a separate story.

And then, just to really make it interesting, he added sound from the studio monitors stationed behind them on tripods, and the inside of the bells glowed in a unique blood red color and with an odd texture.

"Well that does it for my portion of this presentation." he said, chuckled and looked out at his amazed audience. "I shall now turn it over to my esteemed colleague from Tokyo, the fine young Miss Nakanishi."

Soni Nakanishi, the young lady whom had been doing the interpreting as all of this played out – both Japanese to English and English to Japanese – having never missed a beat, smiled demurely, bowed as is formal to Mr. Fujitani and quietly said, "Mr. Fujitani-san and fellow workers on this most wonderful of projects, please allow me to give all of you my findings.

"My expertise is in the verification and authentication of Asian antiquities of art and science. My love - indeed my passion - is finding, verifying and cataloging Japanese and Chinese artworks from the Dynasties of both Imperial Japan and from the eras of Imperial China.

"These bells are beyond intriguing, they are both complex and magnificent. Due to the obvious depth of patina, I first believed them to be of the Ming Era. I was wrong."

She looked around and offered calmly, "It appears that they are the finest and only example we have ever seen that pre-dates Xia, also known as the Hsra Dynasty. That Dynasty was approximately in central China between 2,100 and 1,600 BC. These 'bells' pre-date the CHRIST in excess of 2,000 years – at least!"

Gasps slowly filtered out of everyone's held breaths.

"These bells sing, not just in reality, but they sing the history and the journeys of our people. They include us and combine us in ways that have yet to be told.

"These 'bells' have the following characteristics: they are complex, intricate, goldsmith and gem-smith work of masters quality, coupled with granulation, filigree and inlay, along with a touch of repose, but very little and delicately done. Simply put, they are masterfully understatedly majestic.

"Upon the top of the number one 'bell', and yes they are all numbered with a system that is somewhat Hebrew and part unknown, there is a label - if you will - on its top that identifies it as such.

"As of now, I've only been able to decode the inscription on the top of the number one 'bell'. It is written in a Paleo-Chinese cuneiform that does not match any of the other writings on any of the other surfaces.

"It very eloquently states:

Behold! These are the Imperial Singing Bells known as The Twelve Apostles, passed across the spans of time to our Emperor Ka', the great grandson of King Mu', the grandson of Japheth, one of the three sons of Noah whom was the sole human in his day to be worthy of being called righteous, the great-great-great grandson of Adam whom was the first human being formed from the dust of the Earth by The Divine Breath Of Inspiration. THE CREATOR OF THE UNIVERSE - both in Heaven And On Earth - also known as YAHWEH and GOD ALMIGHTY and IMMANUEL.

"We are the Children of Light and these bells sing our truths immortal."

She left that all sink in, and then added nonchalantly, "And one more item. There is also a lone flaming red dragonfly with both golden wings and golden eyes on the top of the same bell.

"I have one more bit of information gleaned from our studies, due to the well known and infinitely slow buildup and related measured thickness of the patina. These 'bells' predate all other artifacts ever discovered - up until this point in time - by all of mankind." Soni finished, then sat down.

Time stopped in Osaka, Japan. Only the few chosen in the room knew it. The awakening dawn outside heralded it with a spectacular sunrise of deep reds with crisp lines of blue. That daybreak of dawn shook the weary, the wretched, the fools and wise alike into a new day's efforts – yet all those people combined could not begin to touch the efforts being announced, here, in this lab.

Now seated, young Miss Nakanishi continued her startling findings, "The numbering system previously mentioned is as follows," showing a slide overhead: $0 = 0$ $1 = \bullet$ $2 = :$ $3 = /$ $4 = \backslash$ $5 = ---$ $6 = >$ $7 = <$ $8 = \blacklozenge$ $9 = V$ $10 = X$. This system has two items that show up in two separate numbering systems used yet today, the zero for zero and the X for the Roman ten. Somehow those two marks have survived the eons of time.

"As far as I can tell, the inscription on the top that identifies the 'bells', as previously stated, is Paleo-Chinese and thus within my grasp to decrypt and translate. Mr. MIT-sans' projections, cast about the room by his extreme efforts and brilliant methods, are of a language that I have yet to get a grasp of."

She suddenly stopped. The room remained silent for an extended period of time, almost like a wave of exhaustion had entered and permeated into the depths of everyone's final reserves that should have been emptied days earlier.

Mr. Fujitani solemnly asked the two-part question on everyone's minds, "You are saying that these Imperial Singing Bells name both Noah and Adam? Also, that you can not identify the projected language with your obvious skills, and believe me I am impressed to say the least," Then looking around at everyone assembled, "Not just by you, Soni, but also by everyone here. Do you have any theories on what type or style of language may be written upon them?"

Her eyes twinkled. She smiled for the very first time and answered, "Yes I do, Mr. Fujitani-san. I believe based on various factors and characteristics, I think it is an offshoot of Paleo-Hebrew, possibly even predating that earliest form of Hebrew. I have even coined a new name, Pre-Brew!"

And with that, the air that had grown so dense - exploded into laughter – a much-needed break from the heaviness of the subject at hand.

"Pre-Brew! I love that Miss Nakanishi-san! How may we help confirm this wonderful theory of yours?" asked Mr. Fujitani.

"I think we need a Rabbi," she softly answered.

And then, with a longing look and obvious quandary set deep behind her glistening brown eyes, she said, "The original ancient Hebrew – in its primal form - was said to be the language of the angels and the only language that was allowed to be spoken before GOD, in The Realm of the ALMIGHTY in that far distant unknowable place that we call Heaven."

They all slowly filtered out, for a much needed down cycle. Showers, beds, food not from styrofoam containers, and a few days of not interacting at a level that almost made their heads explode.

When they had all left, a very well armed and tightly controlled security detail descended upon the labs. Downloading and copying all data, materials and then packing the 'Imperial Singing Bells' for immediate removal and storage in the Keiretsu's *ichiban* [finest] vault.

Impenetrable and of unknown location, except to Mr. Fujitani and his immediate need-to-know hand-selected personnel.

Mr. Fujitani made it home in the mid-afternoon, got to the highest floors of the ONGCO skyscraper and found his loving, adoring wife. He gave her a hug, laughed and said, "It's time to keep a promise! Time to call Mr. Kealoha-san in Hawaii. Time to take the family and play cowboy!"

She may have never seen him happier, and it lightened her day.

He went to take a shower, barely noticing that it was exactly 3:33 p.m. and that a lot could happen in twelve hours, even the impossible.

When he came out, he looked at the calendar and realized that it was not long before the West's biggest holiday – Christmas. He'd call and see what was appropriate timing to drop in on the Kealoha's world. He could hardly wait to share the knowledge and good fortune of the astounding story of the 'bells'.

And, of course, to ask for one more favor.

15

Higher Power

Mr.Fujitani woke from the most dynamic of dream sleeps, took a shower and looked at the clock. It was 3:33 a.m. – again. He walked out onto the balcony off of his penthouse bedroom suite, slowly closing the door behind him, softly so as not to awake the Missus.

Looking high into the well-lit cityscape sky far above – he simply thought – what have YOU gotten me into? Why would YOU entrust me with such an item as The Imperial Singing Bells, maybe the most valuable artifact of my generation?

He shook his head in frustration and thought – what is it with this Christian GOD? What does he want with me?

And what is it with 3:33?!

Less than 1% of the population in all of Japan declared themselves to be of the Christian faith. Mr. Fujitani was not one of them.

He shuffled back towards bed, better to get back into a time zone that corresponded to his physical location. As he drifted off he was comforted in the knowledge that once the special security detail had left, he alone had stayed behind and switched out the three tiered safe code opening mechanism on the vault door giving it a new protocol for access, an access that only he knew. He'd learned that valuable secret from his father, whom was now buried in Kyoto. His father also taught him that it was impossible to be too careful with two items – assets of extraordinary value and affairs of the heart. These Imperial Singing Bells were turning into both.

*　　*　　*　　*　　*　　*　　*

THE REALM

In The Realm Of Heaven, Noe and Samuel raced at such speeds that when he looked over at her, she was actually just a blur of colors!

They were being pulled by an inextricable force at ever increasing speeds! A Pillar Of Light beckoned them and the sounds of Heaven called!

Looking over, he asked, "What language is that?"

Noe smiled beside him and answered, "Somehow I know that it is the original Hebrew, the language given to Adam and Eve, the language of the angels from before time – the very breath of GOD."

She smiled even more and continued, "Didn't you notice that when I sang to you?"

"I only noticed you." He replied as they sped towards a rendezvous point that got closer and closer and closer.

Then they saw it. On the far side of a distant ridge rising immensely and majestically above the electric green hills nestled in at its feet.

The City Of Gold. The City Of Crystal. The City Of Glass. Glistening golden, covering a huge portion of the horizon! It was awe inspiringly massive and elicited gasps from both Noe and Samuel simultaneously.

What a startling joy to see such a sight! They looked and stared and gained speed and flashed towards their destination, for it had clearly become that. Then, in that instant, Noe was gone! Samuel sped onward, slightly confused and almost sad, but somehow, very deep within, he knew that here, in The Realm, it would be beyond OK.

It would be blessed.

So he just continued racing forward, now alone, but yet with a distant song bursting forth from a multitude of people ... ... not so far now.

* * * * * * *

HAIWIKI RANCH, KOHALA MOUNTAINS, ISLAND OF HAWAII

On a distant hill, in the central Pacific, slightly north of the equator two horses were in love and ran and played and frolicked on lush grass of green rarely checking in on their Earthly masters. One lone tree at the top of the top paddock had become their afternoon retreat. They stayed there in the midday sun. It was evident that the mist and the fog was preferred by both of them. So, as it evaporated and the day came on they lingered under the tree and nuzzled one another.

Mr. Kealoha had saddled up two of the many bays and other paints they kept, along with the 800-plus head of cattle they ran. He wanted to show the Missus where Paint and his new-found love interest went every day.

When they got about two hundred yards out – and upon seeing the horses, they just stopped and looked at the scene before them.

"Those animals are in love." Mr. K. said.

"How cute! He's laying there, and she's kneeling with her head on his neck." She looked at her husband with nostalgia for younger days in her eyes.

"Horse love, what a sight to behold!" then he looked at her and added, "I love you. You are the love of my life."

"That's the type of moment that got us Samuel, you know," laced with melancholy intertwined with a bit of sass. She looked at the two horses and dreamed of days long ago, when in their youth they had a tree like that for picnics and 'such'.

That was early in their marriage, before Samuel, before the ownership of a working ranch, before years of hard toil and before the new now – of deep sorrows – not to be mentioned.

110

16

Redemption Voyage

Grace's small yacht pulled into a tiny village in Palau. She needed just a bit of land time, some provisions, to send a few Christmas post cards and FATHER above had an appointment for her – with whom she was not sure.

She loaded up on what she could, coconuts, dried fish, flower, salt and totally random canned goods. Then she found the post office, and mailed her cards. Went back towards her skiff with her goods, still aware of the lingering final event on her 'to do list'. Just prior to the short paddle in the pristine bay that time had forgotten, here, in ancient Polynesia. Where the only thing that had really changed was the fabric of the clothing and the fact that the women wore two pieces. On the third skiff load, Grace noticed her final obligation, her final joy and the real reason for the land time. Since, after all, she already had enough provisions to reach any destination in the South Pacific.

One young mother with her infant child sat forlorn and crying in a tiny thatched shelter under the shade of the palms at the far end of the beach. She would have been easy enough to miss, but Grace never missed such an opportunity and such a very deep need.

"Hello, my name is Grace," she said in the young mother's native tongue, "Mind if I sit awhile?"

The young girl, probably all of seventeen, looked at Grace, handed the child over and started unloading a lifetime of sorrows, so many harsh burdens for such a young lady. She had been used, forgotten and now ostracized by the very society she thought she'd known. Her father abandoned her, and her mother rarely helped. Life was eating at her very essence, and she was dangerously close to the edge of sanity.

Abandoned, broken, forgotten – she sat here with her baby boy and cried the throws of the weary of heart. She was alone with the only person on Earth whom did not judge her, her baby son.

"Grace is my name – but the grace of GOD ALMIGHTY is what I am here to tell you about. Would you mind if I prayed for you, my sweet and kind young lady?"

She simply nodded the yes of longing hope.

Grace called on GOD for her, spoke life into her, called on prosperity to engulf her in every possible way, blessed her and then gave her a small silken purse for her needs and those of her little boy.

When she was done, the air was more brilliant and a new light shown in the eyes of the young mother who was no longer on the edge of desperation.

Grace paddled out to her schooner without her final skiff full of provisions, she didn't need them as much as her newfound friend did, and she left the confines of the cove for her next rendezvous that would be obvious when she was led there.

After some time enjoying the new found experience of being without all of the weights of the world crushing down upon her, the young lady dared to open the purse and gasped. There was over a year's living expenses held within – along with one tiny note that read, *"GOD loves you – act like it!"*

17

Invitations Of Joy

Mr. Fujitani woke in the middle of the night – seemed like an ongoing ordeal. Shuffling around in his black silk pajamas he once again looked at the results of the bells, astounded he did the mental math and placed a call into his ONGCO office a few floors down – since it was a public utility it never slept – just like him recently. He found his on site operator with English language skills. Using her as a translator, he put a call through to the Kealoha residence.

Mr. Kealoha, heard the phone ring and picked it up. After a brief delay, he spoke to the other side of the Pacific Rim for a brief conversation. Mrs. Kealoha whom was seated next to him heard the following: "Yes, this is he, no, no, no. Yes we would be delighted! Stay with us, no, no – of course – we will see you then. Aloha."

"What in the world was that?" she asked.

"The Fujitanis will be joining us over the holidays, their family plus one. This ought to be interesting!" said Mr. Kealoha to the Missus. "Also he needs to keep the 'bells' a bit longer, maybe even a year. He has a report he wishes to share with us concerning them. But only in person when he arrives."

113

"That's nice. Have they ever had a real Christmas, do you think, Father?" She put her quilting down, having a deep thought on the opportunity to go 'awesome big' for the Fujitani children.

"Doubt it. They are city Nipponese." He smiled, "… and I also doubt that 'Christian' is the box they check when asked for religious affiliation on a form."

They looked at each other and smiled.

Mr. Fujitani, once again getting the extraordinary polite and without hesitation answer he'd wished for, the continued access to the 'bells'. He decided bed would be a good thing and headed that direction. Glancing at the digital clock that was glowing red and hanging on the wall, it read 3:33 a.m., again.

As he drifted off to sleep, he thought to himself, what in the world is it with that number? That has to make at least a dozen times in a row! Seems like the only time I ever see – 3:33 a.m. Then 3:33 p.m. During the past weeks, it was all he saw on the very first glance. How strangely odd … …

Two days later young Miss Nakanishi, looking elegant as ever in a mix of Prada and Armani, walked unannounced into Mr. Fujitani's office, an office of rare and valuable hardwoods; walnut, zebrawood, wenge and curly maples. Scattered around the room were antiquities of the various eras of Imperial Japan, China and Korea along with the prerequisite photo of the family on the desk. Where the family's Samurai Sword had hung was now displayed a Damascus Steel Blade. That blade, of unknown Middle Eastern origin, was not as delicate of a fighting instrument, but certainly every bit as formidable. The only steel superior than what the Samuri masters produced was the lost and forgotten, incredibly sharp Damascus Steel. Created by a master's formula that modern man still coveted and tried to reproduce, yet so far, without success.

"Mr. Fujitani-san, it appears that we have found our Rabbi. He's at Hebrew University in Jerusalem. He teaches ancient linguistics with a bent towards his native language and does research for the nation of Israel on the artifacts recovered from the Temple Mount. Mr. Fujitani-san, his name is Dr. Yurri Goldberg. I have a meeting set for the Monday of next week – if that is approved by you." Miss Nakanishi bowed before him upon completion of the news.

"Go as soon as practical, Soni. This is excellent news – excellent!" He looked at his favorite 'niece' and added, "Please arrive as quickly as you can. Get acclimated prior to your meeting. Jerusalem might be colder than you think."

He smiled and dismissed her to the objective they were both burning to know – of what language was this in reality? And indeed, was it the very spoken word of the angels and a direct connection to the voice of creation and God?

Forty-eight hours later Soni was on her mission via Singapore Airlines. Japan Airways was very nice, Korean Air was excellent, but Singapore Airlines created a whole new level of luxury. She was pampered, fed, then given a hot steaming face towel that the stewardess hand patted to bring the temperature to just perfect. She reclined Soni's seat, lifted her footrest, put on white gloves and proceeded to give her a deep relaxing shiatsu foot massage until she went to sleep. The Earth scrolled by, dreams of Heavenly sounds invaded her soul, and Singapore Airlines had one more, for life, customer.

* * * * * * *

MEDITERRANEAN SEA, TEL AVIV, ISRAEL

When she arrived at Tel Aviv, she felt remarkably fit and ready for duty. She had a few days to get to the meeting up in Jerusalem, so she checked into the hotel and went to sun on the Med with the others who could afford to do so in the middle of the day on the white sands of the sea. Sand with cooking blue skies. Dozens of languages were being spoken all around her, in various dialects and nuances, by people from all across the globe.

For a young language expert – it was as close to Heaven as it could get.

She chose French for the day, and it was glorious!

* * * * * * *

JERUSALEM, ISRAEL

Young Miss Nakanishi was prompt for her appointment at the Hebrew University in Jerusalem. After all, she was Japanese. She'd shopped in some of the upscale boutiques in downtown Tel Aviv, found some more appropriate Mediterranean wear, some really cool shoes and some jewelry to match.

She felt very international, after the office life at ONGCO; it was absolutely liberating.

Expecting to meet with a stuffy elite academic, which she'd been one of while obtaining her own Doctorate. And, expecting a long-winded craggy and wrinkled skin to be the Dr. Goldberg of her imagination, she was startled, stunned more like it, when the secretary escorted her to his office, tapped on the door and said, "Dr. Goldberg, your 10:00 a.m. is here."

Lt. Colonel Dr. Goldberg, Yurri Goldberg, was an officer in the Israeli Air Force whom was in full uniform when he turned and greeted her with a wonderful smile, his hand outstretched and with stunning green eyes brilliance.

Miss Nakanishi, Soni, was left speechless – as was he – both were immediately smitten but too professional to admit it.

Over the course of the next few hours Soni had expected to only disclose the writing with zero back-story. Nothing about the 'bells', their characteristics, their unusual qualities, unknown origin, tonal, octave ranges or about their 'enigma' type status, mysterious materials and methods of construction.

No no no no no …….. all of that went out the door with the brilliant green eyes, radiant smile and hero spirit that resided within Yurri. She gave up all of the bells' secrets willingly, gladly and in explicit detail without a single quamm or moment of hesitation.

After two hours, they got to the four sides of writings and the 'Introduction' on the top of 'bell' number one.

"What type of numbering system is this? It is simple and elegant, and, to me unknown. This alone intrigues me Soni?" He was much more intrigued by her.

"Yes, I understand, the numbering is new to us also. Please notice the only figurine on the entire set, its located on this very surface on 'bell' number one. This lone figurine of a singular dragonfly with its wings in motion, so hard to do! It is clearly visible, yet encapsulated, in both the patina and the diamond outer shell." She smiled at him, then she leaned into him to show him the next high-resolution slide.

"First we thought Ming, then Han, then possibly even Shang. After we determined that this set of Imperial Singing Bells even predated the Xia Dynasty, after discovering the dynamic of the sound coupled with the light activated by pure water, that's when we knew that this language – cast outward by the resonating of the 'bells' singing – was simply beyond us. My theory, Yurri, is that it is possibly one of the oldest known forms of the written word known to man – Paleo-Hebrew. But even then, with unique and subtle variation." She looked at him, softly readjusted her closeness, and with a rather uncharacteristic Japanese sense of humor said, "I've even coined a new phrase – I call it Pre-Brew."

They laughed so hard that it even turned a bit awkward – unprofessional and all – then they lost it again not being able to help themselves.

"Well young lady, being the 'Pre-Brew' specialist Rabbi and all – I'll be the judge of that! May I study these photos of the 'bells' for the day and this evening? I hope this set of prints is for me?" pointing at the glossy fourteen by twenty high resolution set before him.

"Unfortunately we are on maneuvers today, and the military tolerates no absences, even by Rabbis with fancy uniforms and such." He looked at her, then he tried to get back into his 'duty' mode.

"Of course Yurri-san, shall we get back together on the morrow and see where this takes us?" with dancing brown eyes she posed the question.

"Soni, I look forward to our meeting with tremendous anticipation. I shall work on this through the evening and report to you, the Commander of this project, with all of my findings at 10:00 a.m. on the morrow," he said with great formality, standing at rapt attention in his uniform.

She walked over, kissed him on both cheeks a touch longer than needed, turned and walked away. Without a single word she walked slowly away.

The entire conversation had been conducted in French, one of the few common languages they shared, and an international language.

French, a language of nuance, yet more importantly, a language of love.

Maneuvers were tedious for Yurri [the LORD is my light]. And even though Soni's hotel suite had many of the historical sites within easy walking distance, they were of zero interest to Soni. Both could only think of one thing, and that was not the 'bells' or their messages from times long ago. Not the military tactics of modern warfare for Yurri or the Wailing Wall that dominated the Temple Mount only three minutes away for Soni. No, it was the clock that needed to be pressed to 10:00 a.m. the following day – and the fact it would allow them more time with each other.

An eternity passed and 10:00 a.m. could not come soon enough for either Yurri or Soni.

*   *   *   *   *   *   *

"There she is! My lovely lady who I've been waiting for!" Yurri nearly shouted his announcement and hugged her with great enthusiasm.

"Good morning Yurri-san," she stated with typical Japanese formality and hugged back with non-typical Japanese joy.

Yurri laid the photos before them on the boardroom table in the conference room two doors down from his office. "This is fascinating, I can not believe that this has come to me, to us as a nation, from so far beyond Israel and the Middle East. That, in itself, is absolutely extraordinary! What a GOD we serve!" His enthusiasm was contagious and spread to Soni as he continued, "See this lettering. It was hard to place at first. Paleo-Hebrew helped but still allowed for many gaps. These photos of far distant Torahs helped as well and filled in partially, or clarified if you will, fairly large portions of this ancient script – or scroll to be concise. I retrieved some fragments of writing from the earliest known sources. Bits and pieces of scrolls found by Bedouins across Israel and in particular the Dead Sea area and region."

He looked up, smiled and positively glowed with the newfound knowledge he commanded – then said, "And that, my dear, Soni, was the breakthrough! The 'eureka' moment! That's when your numbering system made some sense, for you see ......"

He projected the photos of two fragments onto the wall and held the photos beside them, "... these are not only similar – they match."

He left the discovery settle in.

Soni gasped, her initial judgment was correct and her mind raced with the newfound information.

"Yurri, you genius! Have you really found the primer – the way to decode these projected words from the 'bells' themselves?"

"Yes my dear, Soni, when correlated with these previous bits of antiquity –not only are they translatable – but I have even attempted to solve this first portion. It reads as follows from what you have labeled – 'Bell' Number One North Face. These are the first five lines." He smiled, then projected his translation onto the wall:

Scroll One

"The Song Of Love"

GOD ALMIGHTY – CREATOR OF THE UNIVERSE – KING OF THE ANGEL ARMIES – LORD OF LORDS – IMMANUEL

Sings All Into Creation With Love

They stood there and stared at the projection, the photos and at each other. They were two people that through the years had become so lonely, so bound by structure, duty and endless work. Two souls from vastly different cultures and upbringings. Two souls pressing through barrier, after barrier, after barrier to become the finest in the world at what they had learned, and that which they now did so effortlessly. Both were in their prime, and both, until now, so lonely and desperate for love. Both had an epiphany when they saw the beginning of the words of the ages being revealed before them.

As they stared across the room at the profound projection on the wall and the revelation before them – Yurri simply reached instinctively for her hand – and she did not resist.

By reaching into the furthest recesses of the universe and the dawn of mankind – two souls had found the only real truth of being human, and had found the improbable – each other.

"Wow, Yurri, what do we do now?" She became the little girl deep inside – trusting him with such a simple need.

He picked her up, all 121 pounds of her, twirled her with a huge smile and with great pleasure – and said, "Oh my dear, Soni – I show you Israel! My Israel!"

Then he kissed her right there without hesitation – and from that very moment in time – an elegant fashionable petite city girl from Osaka and a valiant mighty warrior of Israel became inseparable. Melded together by a tremendous force that would not be denied, the first order from the dawn of creation, **LOVE**.

18

The Sea Of Galilee

"No!"

"Yes!"

"Really? That girl always has been more than a little crazy!" said the lower level receptionist to the mail delivery boy at ONGCO's main headquarters in downtown Osaka.

About fifteen minutes later, after the mail delivery boy, whom spoke a smattering of English, had a short and somewhat broken conversation with Dr. MIT that left him in an absolute state of awe.

"She's marrying the Rabbi!" He then told Dr. CMU and his other colleagues in the boardroom that had gathered for a meeting with Mr. Fujitani.

"No!"

"Yes, the Rabbi in Israel! They are getting married – now isn't that something!" said Dr. MIT completely stupefied, the analyst who never did

120

anything in his life unless it was calculated, correlated, calibrated and planned to the nth degree.

"Almost sounds like the punch line to a really good joke, " laughed Dr. CMU, "Now I just have to come up with an excellent beginning for it." Then to no one in particular, "She's marrying the Rabbi! GOD bless her! Doesn't love transcend all?"

Mr. Fujitani walked into the room, looked at the ongoing conversations, very animated conversations, and realized he'd lost control of the meeting before it even started.

After some time passed he got his 'stand in' interpreter's attention, cornered her, and asked what all of the gaijin where so excited about? When he found out, he slumped into his chair at the head of the massive table, looked out over Osaka Prefecture and beyond with a dazed expression.

Finally he got a smile on his face and realized that the feeling he had was the ancient quaint and primal joy of simply being surprised.

He stood up, and in the limited English he commanded, and was trying to learn as fast as possible, stated, "She's marrying the Rabbi! Congratulations for Miss Soni Nakanishi are in order!'

Then with a deep thought, "When?"

The official invitation came to the Fujitani household later that same day via courier. The wedding would be held in Margalit Garden, in Tiberias overlooking the Sea of Galilee in exactly ten days. All were invited, the entire 'bells' working group, fellow co-workers at ONGCO, the Fujitani family – and if Mr. Fujitani would do her the honor – would he be the one to fill in for her father to walk her down the aisle? Her father, some years prior, had finally succumbed from wounds received during the Battle of Saipan.

Of course "If you would be so kind" is exactly how she'd put it to Mr. Fujitani.

Soni had always been like a daughter to the Fujitanis. His family had helped her through school and college, been to every graduation and event for her, and this, her wedding would not be missed.

* * * * * * *

SEA OF GALILEE, TIBERIAS, ISRAEL

Two jets from Osaka with the Blue Flame and Samurai Sword logo arrived in Tel Aviv nine days later. Loaded with passengers and presents and the still amazed look on everyone's faces – she's marrying the Rabbi! An Osaka 'princess', of pure Nipponese descent, marrying an Israeli Jewish warrior. How far beyond the bounds of normalcy could one get?

Their children would be awesome!

The wedding was quaint, reserved, formal, and crisp with all attending being of the highest levels of society spanning four continents. His parents were from southern France, having immigrated to Israel right after WWII to help forge a new nation. Her mother and family were from old Japan – Osaka and Kyoto mostly. The Fujitanis were from Osaka as well. Dr. MIT from Boston, Dr. CMU from Pittsburgh in Western Pennsylvania. Some of the friends were from Oxford, England. Her maid of honor, her best friend since elementary school, was from rebuilt Nagasaki. It was a virtual United Nations convention in a garden setting overlooking the biblical Sea of Galilee.

Communication was a factor, with Japanese being the most difficult language present – followed closely by Hebrew. It appeared from early estimates that French and English would prevail as the languages most usefull to transcend everyone's basic needs.

As formal as the wedding was, the reception was almost out of control! What a tremendous celebration of life! The beer, wine and whiskey all flowed freely. Smiles lit up the surroundings and the music, provided by Yurri's rocking friends, *The Purple Heart Band*, got even the most stoic among them dancing the night away.

It was a sight to behold!

Mrs. Fujitani wanted to know everything, and upon cornering the maid of honor, got the entire story. It appeared that Soni had fallen in love with a true Israeli war hero, courageous among men. He'd been a Lieutenant pilot in an *IDF* fighter squadron when the 1973 Yom Kippur War had broken out. In protecting his homeland, he'd had two jets shot out of the sky within three hours of each other. Parachuting to safety, hitching a ride back to base both times, he'd simply thrown himself back into the fray. Injured and in shock he'd managed to shoot down four enemy aircraft – redeeming himself in the process – and saving the general population of Tel Aviv from a planned bombing run by the Egyptian Air Force.

For those heroic efforts he'd gotten a field promotion to Major and became a living symbol of all that is great about the modern day IDF.

And, of course, he was madly in love with Soni upon sight. Since their first days together they had never left each other's side. How romantic! Even if somewhat scandalous for a girl of pure Nipponese Samurai descent!

Then the maid of honor went on and said, "Mrs. Fujitani-san do you know how he proposed? This is the most amazing part of the story! He took her to some old Roman ruins along the sea, columns standing all in a row as far as the eye could see. He lifted her up onto one of the columns, got down on both knees before her, and, right there said, 'If you will be my loving wife and have the courage to have me as your husband, I will be your mighty warrior and your hero for as long as I live.' He offered her that ring, right there as she stood upon that carved pillar in the fading day's light." She cried with delight when she recounted the story to Mrs. Fujitani.

They looked at each other, held hands and laughed with delight.

Oh how *romantical*!

As the night played on, the people danced, the alcohol flowed and the wild crowd partied in full force. Mr. Fujitani took a good look around and thought – if this is the state of the world today – somehow all will be well.

Seeing the crowd with a different perspective – he thought – the 'bells' are in good hands, no matter the secrets they have yet to reveal. Then one more fleeting thought hit him – Christmas in Hawaii – wonder how that will be?

Before any more cares of the coming days could invade his soul, his daughter grabbed his hand then forced him to forget everything and enjoy a dance with her.

Daughters will do that – it is their right and it is their privilege – it brings a touch of the divine from Heaven to the Earthly Realm below.

* * * * * * *

Overlooking a very late morning's day, sunrise had come and gone long before, the Fujitanis and their companions sat sipping fresh tangerine nectar and eating bagels. Along with coffee, lots and lots of really strong coffee. Soni and Yurri, the newlywed couple, came to see them prior to their journey to the Seychelles Islands. He was going to teach her how to scuba dive. She was going to teach him Japanese in many new and exciting ways.

They were so appreciative and so quaintly cute – what a nice couple – their world would be wonderful. Yet, they were on a mission, a mission of gratitude and also a mission to share Yurri's remarkable findings. He had successfully deciphered, decrypted more like it, the northern face of the Pre-Brew text on 'bell' number one. With Soni's massively qualified help they had transcribed the findings into three languages: Modern Hebrew, English and, of course, traditional Japanese.

Together Soni and Yurri presented to the Fujitani family a rolled sheepskin scroll on olive wood turned handles and hand written in beautifully elegant calligraphy in a very formal script.

The scroll was made as a keepsake for the Fujitanis, but also as a gift for all they had meant to Soni through the years and for all that they had done for her and Yurri as they were starting their brand new lives together.

Mr. Fujitani reverently opened the scroll – looked up at them in awe – put on his formal golden reading glasses, adjusted his posture and proceeded to slowly digest the item in his hands. Not only was it a work of art, but also his hands trembled as he realized the antiquity he held within his grasp. He began to read and got lost in the content of the message sent from times long ago. It went:

<u>Scroll One</u>

"The Song Of Love"

GOD ALMIGHTY – CREATOR OF THE UNIVERSE – KING OF THE ANGEL ARMIES – LORD OF LORDS – IMMANUEL

Sings All Into Creation With Love

Love is the deepest and most abiding force in all that is of creation. It transcends all of creation in every realm. Love simply is. When the very first utterance and command of GOD, CREATOR OF THE UNIVERSE was spoken, it was spoken in Love. Wrapped in Love. Delivered in Love. All that has been, is and forever will be was breathed into its very being by that first divine act of Love. HIS word set the entire essence of all things into the very bedrock of Love.

Love transcends all knowledge, devours all wrongs, builds all that shall be determined to be righteous, absorbs all blows, administers all gifts and divulges – for all to witness – all that is good, pure and beautiful.

Love is obvious. Love is kind. Love knows no boundaries. Love pursues all peoples - until even those whom deny its very existence – until even they must admit its relentless force, a force that shall shatter the very gates of hell and free the captives from within, captives of the deepest darkness and confines shall be saved by the light of Love.

Love abhors indifference and shatters the very souls of those who practice enslavement of the Spirit that GOD has given mortal man.

124

Love shines best when nourished – yet even when put away and left unwanted – breaks away to soar above all wrongs and delivers itself to those most in need of its intimate companionship.

Love is the divine breath of THE ONE AND TRUE GOD, the LIVING GOD, YAHWEH, CREATOR OF THE UNIVERSE and is what makes our Spirits leap, race into an uncertain future as Children of Light and as HIS divines sparks of Love.

Should I speak softly and carry the voice of the angels with the essence of Love within – all things shall be given unto me. The very power of creation shall come forth from my lips and nothing shall be able to withstand my decrees.

Darkness shall flee and the light of Love shall overcome every obstacle.

To speak with the force of Love is to walk in the divine realm of Heaven with the approval of the CREATOR forever across the universe of time.

Love is the original word spoken and shall sing triumphant throughout all of the ages of man.

Love is what binds us

Love is the sound that was spoken at creation

Love is kindness

Love is all that is worthy

Love is what is good, what is clean, what is pure

Love knows only righteousness and truth

Love endures beyond all tribulations

Love shall never end

Love is beyond, above and past time itself

Love can not be crushed or ignored

Love transcends the human mind

Love is fundamental in its existence

Love is existence in its purest form

Love is, that it is, that it is

Love is the light that shines in any darkness

Love destroys the darkness

Love hates that which is evil

Love will not be denied

Love creates the improbable and builds the impossible

Love is the joy in the morning and the hope at night

Love is frailty and crushes that which the world calls strong

Love binds wounds and heals the broken hearted

Love dries the tears of yesterday and tomorrow

Love is life and life will always find a way

Love is GOD and GOD is Love

When all things have passed away

Love will be all that remains

Love is the song of GOD, and that song shall sing forever into the eons of time and through the very souls of man

Sing of Love

Mr. Fujitani rolled up the scroll, then with a knowing smile reached across to his loving wife and handed it to her with a look that spanned the ages. Then he looked at the blissful couple, stood and bowed very deeply, holding the bow for as long as he could. He walked over, clasped both of their hands as one and said, "That is more than I could have ever dreamed! What a marvelous revelation! Wonderful, a gift to the world that we only have but a portion of – after that – what could possibly be on the other three sides?!"

Yurri looked at him, smiled, then he looked at Soni to translate, "I do not know Mr. Fujitani-san, but as for now, with your permission, I have a beautiful bride to take away on our honeymoon. The 'bells' and their songs will just have to wait, for love is calling us today and we shall be back soon enough!" And with that final proclamation he gathered up Soni into his arms, gave a joyous twirl with her feet and hair flying, then swept her down the steps and into a waiting town car below.

Mr. Fujitani sipped on his coffee and pondered, a lighthearted pondering. Mrs. Fujitani read the scroll and cried unabashedly. All the while the children played with make believe angels in the courtyard of the villa – and all was right with their world.

What a fitting place, time and setting to be handed such an ancient truth, such a remarkable treasure of that fact had not been lost on any of the souls present – overlooking the Sea of Galilee where JESUS walked not so long ago.

Mrs. Fujitani – so uncharacteristically of her – came over, sat on his lap and snuggled without a word being spoken.

19

Casting Crowns

Samuel raced to the very presence of JESUS and found himself with HIM, he somehow knew that this is what he'd been racing toward and then drawn to at ever increasing speeds.

Samuel instinctively knelt before his LORD and SAVIOR.

JESUS, without anything but divine love, bowed down and lifted up Samuel before HIM, smiled, then very gently lifted his chin so their eyes met. All things from before flashed all around – Samuel's entire life on display – then rapidly faded as the final scenes played past.

"Samuel Kealoha, you have been found worthy to be written in *The Book Of Life* [book in Heaven listing all who have accepted CHRIST as their SAVIOR], my servant, my joy, my companion, my friend. You have been found to have truth, honor and above all else - courage! Please see the outcomes of your courageous decisions in your life."

What was shown was much more than the three families' rescues. It also showed helping the downhearted being picked upon in grade school. Having the courage to help those who were simply having a bad day – a smile, a kind word

– the little things that so many missed, yet by observation and empathy, Samuel at various times and under many different occasions, did not.

"Oh Samuel, for your heroic deeds, your love and kindness and your strength to overcome – well done, my good and faithful servant!"

JESUS smiled and placed a crown upon his bowed head with all of his acknowledgements and achievements written in glowing words upon its outer rim for all to see.

"Now go, enjoy, explore – live here in the Third Heaven – MY Realm and reign with ME! I am always here, always available for you dear friend."

JESUS, with a joyful glowing smile – cast HIS hand out to show Samuel The Realms' many facets and endless possibilities.

"Oh LORD, for YOU I lay all things down," Samuel said with extraordinary poise as he laid his crown at the feet of his LORD and SAVIOR.

Immediately Samuel found himself sitting at the gazebo across from Noe – stunned to be there – with a complete overwhelming joy along with a bit of relief.

Noe had an awesome spread of exotic fruits and other food items laid out for him, always feeding him it seemed.

A fellow could get used to that.

'I see you don't have your crown," said Noe, holding out a piece of strange fruit with bamboo chopsticks for Samuel to try.

"Felt unworthy to have such a thing in the presence of the only one worthy to wear a crown – especially here." He answered very quietly with great conviction.

"Me, too, never even really looked at mine – tossed it before HIM immediately. Did you see the mountain of crowns all around HIM?" whispered Noe.

"Too busy crying with joy – to be honest!" Then Samuel leaped up – lifted Noe off the bench – twirled her with a huge smile and hearty laugh, and said, "Let's explore!"

Off they raced into their infinite future as Children Of Light.

20

Maui Hold-Em

<u>MAUI RULES</u>

Not open to interpretation

There shall be no female players

Host rulings shall be final and without appeal

There shall be no lending or borrowing of any kind

Deal rotates one human being to the right whom shall call the game of their choice (can not be either an Ohio Game or Trump)

Smoking shall only be allowed down wind

If any player has ever been known to have willingly slept with a dog they must pay double ante for the first hand

All stories must either be told from the truthful perspective or be of such quality as to not matter

Any and all basketball stories shall be limited to no more than thirty seconds upon penalty of death

Upon having exhausted your final monies you must throw your shirt upon the table as to keep yourself into that hand with no further monies due

Each player that exhausts their monies and their shirt shall wear the house provided shirt until exiting the property without exception

At terminal time ending point, from that time forward each hand shall involve the one time ante of the least total of monies held by the poorest remaining player and his shirt

There shall only be ONE WINNER

Finals came and went. Some of The Boys did better than the others. All passed and vanquished the semester to the past. Time for a poker game! Maui was centrally located for all of them, and Kimo filled in as both host and a way to fill the voids of Timmy, and now, Samuel.

"So what's the designated activity? Nice! I'll bring my mask." Nalu hung up from the call. Kimo decided diving would be a good thing; he had arranged for a dive boat, dive master and all of the gear – although most of the guys would probably bring their own mask, fins and snorkels, especially the mask since it was such a personal and intimate item. The wrong mask could quickly ruin a dive.

William, Johnny and Jesse were not certified, thus the need for the dive master. She was a tall, long-legged blonde with a wire attitude and an easy presence about her.

On the ride to the 'Lobsterminiums' on the far side of Lanai, where towering brown seacliffs that had steps of broken lava formations creating underwater shelves stepping downward into the rich blue abyss below. They were riddled with small caves that lobsters, in great abundance, thrived in.

Jolene [brilliance, strength], the dive master for the day, gave her blunt and pointed instructions. Safety! Safety! Safety! – she walked them through the gear, the dive tables, the dive profile, the timelines, the valves, troubleshooting, the essence of 'the buddy system' and all of the other nuances to being under water with compressed gasses as your only lifeline. They were to follow her. And, no matter what, they could do almost anything – but go up fast!"

"NEVER – EVER – EVER – GO UP FAST!" Jolene ordered.

Her brilliant instructions, delivered with both poise and knowledge, landed on the dullest sets of ears she would ever, in her life, encounter.

Proof of that would be self evident in minutes.

With the boat squarely anchored, Akina, Nalu and Makani immediately grabbed their spears, stringers and bags then disappeared into the depths below headed toward the 'Lobsterminiums'. Intricately hollow cathedral formations stepping down into the deep blue abyss just off the thousand foot seacliffs.

William, Jesse and Johnny – the novices extraordinaires leaped into the water just as Jolene was going to check and re-check their gear.

"Too late for that! There they go!" she called out to the boat captain and no one in particular. Then she dove in after them.

Johnny, who had his air on and strong fins, went straight down into the blue – trailing a long streamer of bubbles and nothing else. No 'buddy system' today – not for Johnny anyways.

William went a completely different direction, disappeared around the boat to the south, and then was gone from her sight within seconds.

It was Jesse whom really screwed up. He'd done the zero check on gear thing and was now experiencing the 'Shaka – one, two, three and you are dead scenario'. First he'd failed to turn on his air tank, second he'd not been able to inflate his *Bouyancy Compensator* [BC], and third he'd stepped off the boat into 600 feet of water and was now sinking fast. When Jolene the dive master got to him, he was at 80 feet and plummeting. He'd been trying to clear both ears but was starting to have real problems with them as they were giving him sharp jabs of pain like never before. She caught him at 80 feet, stopped him at 90 feet and got him settled into actually breathing on his own at 100 feet. She grabbed him by his straps, face to face, Jesse half terrified and her half smoking. She swam him back to the surface, inflated his BC, and told him under no uncertain terms, "Stay put!"

Then she found William, who had discovered a quirky nuance to the gear that was not in the owner's manual. He'd swim down to about 20 feet then rapidly inflate the BC, and kicking as fast as possible, see how much air he could get when he breached the surface! He was having a gloriously fun time getting almost completely out of the water when Jolene caught him on the surface of one of his 'rocket launches'. She grabbed him and scolded him like he hadn't been scolded since he was five. She latched onto him without an inch of 'polite tour guide', and more like a 'shock collar' on a bad dog, swimming him over to hang on the surface, in shame, with Jesse.

Then Jolene went looking for her third charge, Johnny. She spotted him by seeing a rising stream of bubbles from the depths over where the others were blue water hunting. At 120 feet, the bubbles coming past her were the size of the hood on her Datsun 240 Z! She dove faster and caught Johnny inside a small cave at 204 feet offering his regulator to a fish, being polite enough to ask the fellow cave dweller it if needed a breath of fresh, human compressed gas? He was *narced* out of his gourd and 150 feet deeper than he should have ever been.

Nitrogen narcosis [drunk feeling] was a reality and *the bends* [compression sickness] was a distinct possibility. As she swam him to the anchor line she did the mental math, hung him off the anchor line at 60 feet, sprinted to the surface, grabbed two bottles of air, switched him out under water with just 35 psi left in his tank, and then switched hers with less than 100 psi in it. She made him linger for forty minutes, just gawking around, until he'd bled his blood nitrogen levels back to the proper ratio to sustain life and not explode all of his tiny little blood vessels.

Akina, Nalu and Makani all had an absolutely wonderful time enjoying the heck out of their two-tank dive. Between them they got 40 *menpachi*, 2 *scorpion fish*, 1 large *popio*, 1 medium *kohala* and 22 big lobsters – a couple of the lobsters were over seven pounds – none of them were under three and a half.

After the scolding that William, Johnny and Jesse got – their day wasn't nearly as fun.

* * * * * * *

HISTORIC TOWN OF LAHAINA, ISLAND OF MAUI

As for Jolene, the babe of a dive master, she never said another word after her final venting, and as they rounded the point into Lahaina Harbor, she was the first to disembark.

Going straight to the dive shop she immediately resigned by photo copying her middle finger, signing it and dating it!

In her mind, stewing the entire time, was one overriding thought – local boys ………….. they are all crazy!

Kimo picked them up at the dock and asked, "How did it go? Sorry I had to work."

He got three thumbs up and three thumbs down.

On the way back to Maalaea, Kimo pulled over and stopped at a ramshackle house with one huge mango tree on the backside of it. Kimo scooped up many of the fish and half a dozen lobsters into two large baskets. Took them with him and knocked on the door. A weathered, battered by life, lady opened the door with an apron and two children clinging to her.

'Yes, how may I help you, Kimo?" she asked in a worn out voice.

'Auntie, we've got some extra fish – mind if we drop some for you? A few lobsters, too, Auntie." He smiled and asked, "Care to trade for a few mangos off your tree out back?"

"Wow, good trade for Auntie," William said none too happy.

"No William, good trade for us. Judging from what you, Johnny and Jesse survived today, at least one good deed was in order. " He gave a look to William that shut him down, and the subject was never broached again.

133

A lone blue dragonfly of unknown origins flew onto the porch of Auntie's house, then eyed the mango tree, and headed that direction.

* * * * * * *

Kimo took all of the money, flight coupons and t-shirts that night – and deservedly so – it was not beginner's luck.

21

Beams Of Light

Back on the Earthly Realm, Christmas was invading the world and even Hawaii Nei had its own unique methods of celebration.

Palm trees decorated like a Dr. Seuss drawing, and Santa wore shorts at the mall.

Upon the lush winter green hills of Kohala under fog drip and downpours, sunshine composed of walking beams of light danced to and fro. The horse, Paint, and the Arabian had become inseparable; they craved each other's company minute by minute.

"If I didn't know better, Mother, I'd think that that Arabian was with foal."

"Maybe we've got our first Christmas miracle! Better call Doc Vet and have her checked. If she's with baby, we'll need to change her diet a bit and watch her at least half as much as Paint does."

"If she's pregnant, we'll have to change his name from Paint the Pony to Paint the Stud!" he chuckled.

"Father!" she whacked him, actually rather hard, then went back inside to make more Christmas cookies for the Fujitani family arriving later in the day and for their appointed Christmas Eve-Eve rounds, their in-house nickname for December 23rd.

135

* * * * * * *

KONA AIRPORT, KEAHOLE POINT, ISLAND OF HAWAII

Once again the ONGCO Gulfstream II landed at Keahole Airport on the barren lava flats, touching down in calm conditions at 154 kts, and screaming to a stop without regard for the crazed sea birds fishing along the jagged rock shoreline. Aama crabs ignored all and scavenged what they could, unaware of the one lone mongoose. It was looking for a different meal and adapting rather well to ocean front living. It snagged a large startled jet-black crab in its jaws then ran into the scrub kiawe nearby. Two pincers gripped the mongoose on one cheek, but it was as tough as its native India, and it just bit all the harder. She dropped her catch into the small den of her broad of young that immediately ravished the black arachnid into shreds that they fought over to the last morsel.

This mongoose Christmas feast involved seafood, and thus, was typically Hawaiian.

* * * * * * *

HAIWIKI RANCH, KOHALA MOUNTAINS, ISLAND OF HAWAII

Once again, the Fujitani clan climbed up the far hills of Kohala in a white limousine, instead of them being five plus one, now, with the impromptu wedding upon the shore of the Sea of Galilee, it was plus two. Soni and Yurri were with them, for they had graciously accepted to join them and translate as needed. Mr. Fujitani had been trying to 'force learn' some English, for a man of his age bracket, his learning curve was admirable, but far from being of much use.

"Mr. and Mrs. Kealoha-san, thank you so much for inviting us to your wonderful Christmas! Wow! This is gorgeous!" said Soni, losing her formality with an awe that couldn't be hidden.

Haiwiki Ranch and their ranch hands had spared no expense and had wanted to show their very best for these friends that had traveled so far to be here.

White lights trimmed every single building's eaves, windows and rooflines. The walkways had green lights on every side. Each tree was in deep reds and blues to offset and soften the square edges. One lone bottlebrush pine was decorated in various colors, tinsel, ornaments and a multitude of decorative presents scattered all around with one lone crystal star glowing brightly on top. Shining a light of hope to all around.

But the best, the coup de gras, a huge pile of snow, freshly brought down from Mauna Kea, accented the house with newly sculpted Frosty and Frostyette adorned in lights! He with a pipe and her with a spatula stood majestic and glistening as they melted slowly in the evening's fading light.

The Fujitani children sprinted to the snow, fell into it and made snow angels as they got relief from such a long journey.

Then, at the exact perfect moment, when all was right with the world, one of the ranch hands brought an old buckboard, retrofitted to seat eight, around the corner all lit up with blue and white lights highlighting its every edge. Even the horses had lights on them to add to the magical experience.

Presents flowed in heaps in the back – presents for the shut-ins that the Kealohas rode to every Christmas Eve-Eve and delivered a touch of Heaven to their hard existences for the elderly and indigent in the village down below.

* * * * * * *

PLANTATION VILLAGE OF NIULII, DISTRICT OF NORTH KOHALA, ISLAND OF HAWAII

They rode the wagon down the driveway to the little village known as Niulii, a group of tightly packed small homes on stilts, a camp from the sugar era. Third generation now; intermingled and morphed to be Japanese, Filipino, Portuguese. Interspersed with hippies, retirees and such. Mostly getting along wonderfully, but not without a few ruffles and tribulations, both large and small.

First stop was for a widow of about ninety. She was given cookies, a couple small presents and bread. Canned goods and a gift card at the local store to help her with groceries for all of the coming year. Stops two through eight were for families struggling with being able to buy their children presents of any kind, who lived in broken homes for one reason or another, by either circumstance or dysfunctional parents that could not handle adulthood and fell short in many ways.

The Kealohas did not judge, just showed GOD's love in a straightforward fashion. It was Christmas and all keikis needed a touch of kindness.

Stop number nine was the local church, where they made a sizable donation and left the remaining presents for the priest to distribute as he would.

Stop number ten was at Niulii Cemetery, where the parents of the late Samuel Kealoha, placed a wreath made of maile and pikake upon the cross that marked an empty grave.

Mrs. Kealoha left one of Samuel's favorite cookies on that cross, while Mr. Kealoha pressed a golden coin firmly into the ground, out of sight to all others.

After some time, they walked back to the waiting electric ensemble and rode, singing Christmas carols, back to the ranch high above, now glowing in the deepening black of a star cast sky arching from Heaven to Earth.

* * * * * * *

HAIWIKI RANCH, KOHALA MOUNTAINS, ISLAND OF HAWAII

Mr. Kealoha taught the children how to make snowballs as the last of the snow vanished. Then he taught them how to make 'smores' over the fire as everyone ate a massive meal of lamb, steak, ulua and lobster. Way too many types of desserts had been placed out: carrot cake, mountain apple pie, mango crisp and all things Christmas – Hawaiian paniolo style.

The evening lasted forever as the fire burned on and the families from all over the world congregated as one and sang songs of hope and good cheer. Red wine for the Goldbergs, beer and sake for Mr. Fujitani and Mr. Kealoha, punch for the children and fresh squeezed tangerine juice mixed with champagne for Mrs. Fujitani and her friend across the great language divide Mrs. Kealoha. All together it lightened the mood for everyone as sparks shot upwards towards Heaven, a Heaven that briefly invaded a small speck of Earth below with the experience – for many the first time – of what a true and joyous Christmas should be.

It was Christmas Eve-Eve, and the most wonderful was yet to come.

Mr. Fujitani woke in the middle of the night, his family was the guests of the Kealohas and stayed in the cottage that was clean, had new sheets, a multitude of homemade quilts, a small woodburning Ben Franklin cast iron stove, drinks and fruits and crackers and cheese in the fridge. Three children completely passed out and snuggled in futons on the floor around the king sized koa bed that he shared with the jetlagged mother of his children.

He walked out on the lanai after glancing at the clock – lit by fire – and seeing 3:33 a.m. once again. That time phenomena half freaked him out but deeply intrigued him as well.

When he walked outside, he saw Mr. Kealoha, as himself, was up and awake sitting on the lanai of the ranch house sipping on one last beer – an *Asahi Super Dry* of all things. He offered one to Mr. Fujitani without saying a word. They sat for some time. Together they silently watched a lone fireball light up the sky above. It tumbled and broke apart over the Pacific to the distant northwest.

"Mr. Kealoha-san I am so sorry about Samuel. Your son had courage like no one else I've ever met," Mr. Fujitani said matter-of-factly in broken, but yet very understandable, English.

"I miss him, every day – every single day. Yet here you are, and two other families as well – and for that I am grateful. Samuel, much like that shooting star, shed his light for those who needed to see it." It was the first time he could articulate a few of his deeper thoughts concerning his only son.

"Mr. Kealoha-san, every day and every night I keep seeing, at first glance on the clock, the same numbers – three three three – I am at a loss why? A great mystery to me, Mr. Kealoha-san! A great mystery?"

Walking across the lanai and slowly opening the door, then arriving back and standing in the glow from the night light filtering out of the kitchen window – Mr. Kealoha opened a well worn family Bible for Mr. Fujitani to see. He opened it to Jeremiah and softly read out loud, slowly for Mr. Fujitani to grasp the very essence, the very Word of God as written so long ago:

'Call unto me, and I will answer thee, and show thee great and mighty things, which thou knowest not. ' [Jeremiah 33:3 KJV]

He closed the Bible, and they both pondered the immensity of the universe laid out before them in the stars above and in the Holy Scriptures passed down through the eons of time.

Generation upon generation upon generation.

* * * * * * *

Just because it was the morning of Christmas Eve meant little to the critters on the ranch. Gertrude and her chicken compatriots still clucked and laid five findable eggs. Nasty Kyle, the escapee bani rooster, still acted with total arrogance toward all things and at least had the meanness to keep the centipedes under control along with his harem of hens. Katt the Cruiser cruised and never lifted a paw to help in any way. Dogg literally was the welcome mat and was still breathing – apparently. Mr. Kealoha noticed all of the refugee critter's activities, sighed and went down to the lower paddocks to open a few gates. His herd could, at their leisure, navigate into another section of the ranchland to find more feed and try and knock the grass down a little bit. He did a rough count to make sure that the herd hadn't escaped through a hole in the fence and into the jungle beyond.

All appeared well, it was 6:54 a.m., the sun was barely peeking over the mountains above, crispness was dominating the air and there was not a cloud in the sky. Heavy dense dew saturated all things with a freshness of breath from Heaven.

Mr. Fujitani with two of his three children in tow, found Mr. Kealoha in the barn as dawn moved all people to rustle alive – regardless of their internal clocks – on a working ranch the external goings on trumped everything, even jet lag.

Mr. Fujitani was in awe, maybe more in shock, as he saw what had become of his treasured family sword, the last Samurai sword of the Fujitani-ya Clan – a Masamune Super Blade! The soul of the family patriarch! An irreplaceable museum quality masterpiece that had been wedged unceremoniously into the barn beams and was now being swung full force to cut binder twine on hay bales! By Mr. Kelaoha – gaijin!

How awkwardly strange!

Mr. Kealoha saw the 'aghast look' on Mr. Fujitani's face. Saw it for what it was – and went full blooded American on him. He dragged down another hay bale, laid it out before Mr.Fujitani, and handed him the sword.

Mr. Fujitani had never seen "The Masamune" unsheathed, let alone used for farm chores, and could barely grasp the event unfolding before him.

Mr. Kealoha smiled and nodded at the hay bale, then moved the children back a few more steps.

With great trepidation, Mr. Fujitani took the classically trained *Kendo* [martial art] stance, then with one swift motion cut the first strand of binder twine, then slowly and very stylized, cut the second.

A faint smile ran across his face.

Mr. Kealoha rolled a second hay bale before him. Mr.Fujitani, with much more gusto, cut the twine on it as well.

Ten more bales and a fairly large stack of second crop alfalfa piled up, more than enough for the horses to munch on for the week ahead.

With that, Mr. Fujitani was a liberated man! Dragged out of the world of dogma and duty and into the world of the living! Not remaining a slave to traditions, things or ideologies – all simply by wielding an ancient symbol of entrenched Japanese structural traditions as a farm tool – and having immense fun while doing so!

Mr. Kealoha thought that Mr. Fujitani had potential after all.

Mrs. K. had blueberry muffins, butter, guava jam and fresh Kau coffee laid out on the kitchen counter for all to share. Along with some tangerine juice for those that needed some condensed sunshine instead of Kau coffee rocket fuel running in their veins at this time of day. Over the course of the next twenty minutes, the humans started joining the land of the living and catching up with the critters. Paint and the Arabian ambled over and started working on some of the fresh alfalfa put over the fence just for them.

Soni, cradling a cup of coffee, started to explain in Japanese the coming days' events. "We are all to get ready for a journey and picnic at the upper reaches of the ranch via jeep and horseback to see a very special place. Appropriate clothing would be essential. Long pants, shoes and some sunscreen would be needed, a good attitude would be a blessed thing as well!" she added with a smile.

* * * * * * *

HOKU FALLS, WAIMANU VALLEY, SEVEN VALLEYS OF THE KINGS, ISLAND OF HAWAII

A menagerie of five Fujitanis, two Kealohas, two Goldberg newlyweds and some light lunch items made its way to the top reaches of the ranch and a trailhead at the furthest top gate. From there, with the jeep parked downhill in case it needed help starting, and the horses left to roam in the fifty acre enclosed paddock, the group of explorers trudged along the one mile jungle trail.

Eating stray guavas as they saw them, finally around the last bend and right before them, they arrived at their destination – the very back of Waimanu Valley. Waimanu's deepest secret and wildest closely guarded vista – where *Hoku Falls* [Star Falls], a 2,770 foot plus waterfall resided. Their trail terminated onto a small shelf with a pool of green that was at the 1,150 foot mark on one of the largest freestanding waterfalls on the planet. The tiny stream fell so far that it became a heavy mist – literally turning back into rain – wavering about by a kind gentle breeze and showing glimpses of rainbows as the light danced through it.

All was encased in a million shades of green, dark chocolate and black outcroppings of barren lava. Ferns grasped at the vertical sides and gave a soft edge to the majestic falls in the very intimate presence of the stunned visitors whom had never seen such a place and thought that they only existed in movies and fantasy.

Mr. and Mrs. Kealoha held each other and allowed the views and experience to speak for itself.

Soni and Yurri held each other tightly, Mr. and Mrs. Fujitani stood in stunned amazement while their children jumped up and down and screamed into the valley below that ran far away to the blue ocean in the distance.

By the time every one of the newcomers had the scenery sink into their psyches, Mr. Kealoha had everything delivered to Mrs. Kealoha who had the picnic all laid out. After all, it was Hawaii and Christmas Eve. Why in the world would you not feast?!

Children the world over never miss a chance to throw rocks, and this was an awesome rock throwing opportunity. You couldn't even see them land they fell so far! Pretty soon everyone was throwing rocks except for Mrs. Kealoha and Mrs. Fujitani who sipped homemade iced tea with swizzle sticks of fresh cut sugarcane and enjoyed the fact that happiness had invaded their worlds. No translation was necessary.

* * * * * * *

HAIWIKI RANCH, KOHALA MOUNTAINS, ISLAND OF HAWAII

On Christmas morning, with the tree lit and fresh coffee and fruits on the ever-stocked kitchen counter, the children had their first taste of a real Christmas – ever!

Mrs. Kealoha read the Christmas story from Luke in the Bible; Soni translated with a joyful reverence.

Presents were exchanged, a multitude of toys, blue jeans and cowboy hats for the kids. They all got belts from hand cut strips of leather, tooled and adorned with the Circle HR Brand made from brass for the buckles.

Mr. Kealoha handed to Mr. Fujitani a handmade, notch mitered and jointed box made from the finest double standing wave patterned koa that appeared three dimensional by the cross hatched optical illusion within its grain. The top was of 'gold koa', the sides were of 'black koa', all dovetailed together to add maximum contrast. Inside was lined with deep rich burgundy velvet, and on that lay a belt buckle with the same Circle HR Brand created in burnished brass.

Mrs. Kealoha handed Mrs. Fujitani a package, that when opened, revealed a queen sized Hawaiian quilt of various pinks, whites and blues. It had a snowflake motif with an overlay of Bird of Paradise hand stitched into it.

Seeing that Soni and Yurri were there – and always anticipating a few extra souls at this time of year – they had a similar quilt and box for them as well.

All of the items spoke of hours upon hours of extreme craftsmanship.

Having been informed of the 'gifts custom' associated with a traditional American Christmas, the Fujitanis presented one single gift to the Kealohas; it was for both of them. Once the very beautiful wrapping paper was removed by Mrs. Kealoha, a black lacquered box emerged, with the finest inlays of golden trees and flowers. They opened it together and found a scroll with walnut turned handles and hand writing in the most elegant flourish of calligraphy of deep rich black ink on paper made of the finest methods. When revealed, it was 'The Song Of Love' from the Imperial Singing Bells.

Soni and Yurri very excitedly, and with much hand waving animation, explained what they were holding and the back-story of what all the 'bells' had revealed to date.

It was Mr. and Mrs. Kealoha's turn to sit in stunned amazement – all of that from the 'bells' that sang lullabys for them to sleep when it rained – who would have ever thought such a thing?!

* * * * * * *

HAPUNA BEACH STATE PARK, ISLAND OF HAWAII

By noon, they were all down the mountain and playing in the perfect tiny waves at Hapuna Beach, getting some sun and enjoying crystal blue waters at a very relaxing pace.

Only on the Island of Hawaii could one lounge in eighty-six degree water of turquoise joy and see snow on two mountains softly adorning the ambiance of a wonderful summer's Christmas Day.

Everyone said their goodbyes at the beach. The Fujitanis were going to settle into the Rockefeller Resort – one of the Keiretsu had a house there and it was made readily available with both chef and butler for them. The Kealohas were headed back up the mountain to ranch living and to read the scroll that so intrigued them.

Then they would take a much-anticipated nap, after all, guests can really wear you out!

Samuel, their only son, was so deeply missed but as they looked into that scar within the backs of their eyes, that was seared into their very souls, not a word was spoken. Not a word.

22

Quest For Eden

Soni and Yurri politely ditched the family and went to Hilo for a little more honeymooning and to enjoy a side of the island they'd never seen except for photographs on postcards. East Hawaii had white sand tidal pools, black sand beaches, Volcano National Park, Japanese gardens and the best sushi on Earth. But the company of each other would be the true joy, without any needed translation of any kind.

Two days later, they purchased a twenty-acre oceanfront point of land along the Hamakua Coast just north of Hilo Town – cash. They pried it away from a local company, *Sugar Mountain Lands*, by offering a premium price. The land was awesome with views all the way down the coast to Hilo and beyond.

Just because he was an Israeli Officer and she was a linguistics and antiquities expert didn't mean they were poor, in fact just the opposite, for they both had acquired real wealth by excellent investing and being willing to take risks. When they saw that piece of land jutting into the vast blue Pacific – they knew they had found home – and a place to build a new life, in peace, together.

Over the course of the next five weeks they had a local operator use a massive *Caterpillar* D9 bullozer to clear the California grass, guava and stray sugi pines from the property, exposing the richest top soil on Earth. It was twenty-two feet deep, loamy, volcanic, ultra-rich, 'grow anything' type of dirt. Fruit trees, researched relentlessly by Yurri, were obtained to plant a five-acre orchard.

Lychee, mango of various types, rambutan, star fruit, avocado of six varieties, Chinese banana, mountain apple and a small stand of the guava left along the gulch for canning. Macadamia nut trees edged everything in two-tree deep borders.

Beautiful four-rail white fencing with an interior of woven wire encircled the entire property's farming portions to accent it all. Royal Palms were planted on both sides of the ¼ mile driveway to the dozed pad created to build their home upon. It was for the *Ohana* [family] house, or guesthouse, giving them a place to grow from. They hoped to eventually build a much larger formal main home – but they couldn't agree upon what it should be yet and weren't able to envision the house of their dreams at this stage.

With those improvements over the five week period, they had a fledging orchard, pasture land started, a house pad, a driveway entrance rough landscaped and had found a Japanese groundskeeper and landscaper whom was better at Hawaii foliage and design than they would ever be.

They saw that it was coming together nicely, so they declared victory on phase one.

Soon they returned to Japan's industrial city of Osaka. Their true mission called, and the 'bells' drew them back to the deep mysteries that were held within and had not been identified yet – or even dreamed of.

23

Osaka Sings

Dr. MIT and Dr. CMU and the newlyweds had all reconvened at the secret lab. All had had their holidays with their families, all enjoyed the divergence from the tediousness of applied laboratory methodologies, and all had needed a break. Yet, every single one of them desired to get back to the tasks at hand.

Soni and Yurri went straight to decrypting the remaining three sides. The South, East and West faces of the 'bells' and the songs they believed were contained upon them.

Substantially more than expected had been found upon the North face, 'The Song Of Love'. There were twelve 'bells' and all twelve having a portion of the song upon their exteriors, and now, the encoded primer gave them the proper order to arrange them in, 'The Song Of Love' truly 'flowed' and came together as enlightenment passed down from ages past.

Now they could do their best with the other three faces and hopefully yield similar results.

Dr. MIT was absolutely fascinated with the mechanism on how the 'bells' 'sang'. What was the key to the resonance? Why only pure water and natural sunlight? Why and how did the encased diamond function at certain octaves and corresponding flow rates? Why? Why? Why? Answers were becoming hard to quantify, certainty was lacking, but any changes of either flow rates or projected pitch and volume levels created a myriad of results. All needed to be cataloged and investigated. All facets of the work were more than intriguing; they were mesmerizing for a man of his background.

Dr. CMU was just as thrilled with the historical and now the actual decrypted passage of the north face of the twelve bells. The language, 'Pre-Brew' fascinated him. Complex structure with definitive meanings, deep subtleties all on the 'bells' that defied any means of mechanical construction?

Diamonds that were the size of grapefruits, sapphires the size of hockey pucks – shaped, faceted and bonded into one singular resonating bell. Not just once, but also twelve times matching, all tuned together and all tuned separately.

And what on Earth is that deep indigo glow coming from the inside of the 'bells'? The thoughts of all of the world-class investigators lingered on that one question and that question begged for an answer. Are these bells or are these 'bells' a device?

Dr. MIT was puzzled by the simplicity of the 'bells' and the complexity that came from them; it more than fascinated him. He had been taught so many complex methods, actually had been on the leading edge in developing more than one of them to allow for measurements, dating and quantifying various objects, machines and such, from all around the world. From ancient clocks and weapons of war to ultra modern engines and instruments. He'd seen, held and deciphered items of antiquity and helped design the cutting edge items of the modern era.

But at these 'bells' he simply stared and pondered – for hours. At times in a state of awe. Other times in a sheer frustration.

Inspiration can be like a lightning strike, so fast and fleeting that if you don't act upon it immediately you may forever miss the brief glimmer of the divine that just flashed through your brain. Like a fogged dream, not quite able to put it back together as originally fabricated deep within the human spirit.

He kept arranging his 'bell' photos on his desk in shapes until he finally saw it! Startled at his thought, he leaped up out of the worn leather office chair that had become his best friend, sprinted over and grabbed a fresh stack of high-resolution photographs of the profile of all twelve 'bells'. With scissors in hand, he worked at cutting each profile out of the photos one by one.

They had hung the bells, as originally found, they had hung the bells side by side, they had hung the bells in a circle, and in every instance, the results were amazing, but yet the same.

But what the Dr. from MIT had grasped was the obvious that had eluded them for so long – the bells of a slightly conical shape all had thirty degree sloped faces on every side. And with the top 'connector' that was on top facing in, and with all twelve bells arranged in a tight circle, they all fit into a perfect wheel. Tight with zero space or gap between them they fit as one! With the primers well known, the numbers in order, you had four distinct proper fits of 1-12 N, 1-12 S, 1-12 E and 1-12 W. In each case, the ring holders on top, offset slivers of an unknown material overlapped as a single circular match point or axis.

These were not bells, well, of course they were individually, but together they were a device. A device of magnificently inspired craftsmanship. A device of unknown origin. A device of unknown usage, and until now, of unknown design. Until now!

"A device!" he yelled to his colleagues, all who had stopped the relatively important work they'd been doing to focus squarely on the Dr. from MIT who was acting possessed and playing with the 'bells' like tinker toys in the clean room.

When he stood back and showed them the design and device laying on the table before him, they all gasped – stood still – then applauded him and his findings with loud clapping and some good old fashioned hooting and hollering.

As a pale quiet set in once again, Yurri, the newlywed Rabbi, said in Pre-Brew, "Well done, my good and faithful servant, well done!"

Only Soni understood. She was becoming a quick study in all things Hebrew.

Out of the corner of his eye, Mr. Fujitani, who had just briefly stopped in, saw the time on the wall. It was 3:33 p.m.

Of course it was!

Deceivingly simple puzzles are, at times, the very hardest of all. Mocking those who look for that which is not missing, the obvious 'hiding in plain sight' right before their very eyes.

24

Rendezvous

Four weeks earlier and far far away, in the land of misty mountains and people from all walks of life, 'The Boys' – Samuel's friends – got together for one last poker game before 1976 exited to the annals of history as the year of tremendous changes – mostly good – but with the loss of Samuel, a year of sorrows unimaginable.

Nalu called *The Boys*. The activity would be New Year's Eve in Waikiki, which alone would be more than enough. Maui Hold-Em to follow, at high noon on the very first day of 1977. It would be an excellent way to bring in a New Year: friends, beer, football and poker. Doesn't get any better than that!

Nalu, Jesse and Akina left the Diamond Head residence to the other guys that chose to hang out with the over anxious girls and a thousand varieties of mixed drinks on the counter and on the floor. Grabbing two mopeds and one pedi cab loaded to the gills with fireworks, they migrated to Kapiolani Park and set up for the initial go-round with the pyrotechnics at their disposal. They proceeded to blast some roman candles into the gathering haze of cordite and suspended debris filled atmosphere. Their display blended into the ever-approaching midnight's flashes of brilliant colors going off all around them.

Waikiki, Honolulu and Oahu in general looked more like a Chinese Hong Kong event, a completely out of control chaos of overlapping blossoms of fire. More than anywhere else in America!

Chaos reigned everywhere in three dimensions – four if you counted sound. Even the children, way too loose and young, got in on the act. They spun and ran amok with wild abandon, twirling sparklers and throwing ladyfingers provided by their drunken uncles and aunties, who were brought up exactly the same way.

At 11:30 p.m., the three headed into the heart of the ongoing onslaught of the senses – Waikiki proper. Hotels - twenty, thirty and forty stories tall had fire rushing down their sides onto the sidewalks below. Hotel guests and employees, all with keys to the roofs and liquor cabinets, threw, shot and flung all types of fireworks from their lofty perches onto the sidewalks and everything else below.

Strings of 500 and rolls of 1,000 firecrackers were lit and launched at the cars below – exploding with ever increasing ferocity as they self immolated, spiraling by gravity, and explosions lighted the night with white-hot flashes. Giving the view below of being an endless burst of strobe lights, like a million welding torches gone crazy.

Tourists ran and screamed as they left one bar for another, one hotel for another, one sense of false shelter for another.

Nalu, Jesse and Akina – knowing to leave the mopeds and pedi cab chained in the relative safety of the park – tore into the mess with wild joy. Screaming, going from overhang to overhang, and trying to make it to the big Rock and Roll party being drowned out by explosions at *Duke's Bar and Grill.*

Might as well dance there with the other thousands of people who couldn't hear the music either!

At ten minutes 'til midnight and two blocks from Duke's – with all of their fireworks finally exhausted - they hid under the awning of a business across from Wall's Surf Break. That's exactly when crazy reached a whole new level of WOW FACTOR! Now the firework explosions were seamless, the smoke became overwhelming in the stagnate air and chaos reigned supreme. All of the cars stopped on the Boulevard, most by choice, but all by forced necessity. Every road was blocked by the crazy calm of motionless traffic trapped in a sea of explosions gone mad, rocket launches and random raining sparklers. Everyone was on the inside of a fireworks factory explosion! Most hid like the three friends were, yet some got trapped in the open and needed shelter immediately, more than they ever had in their lives.

That is exactly when Nalu saw her, capturing his complete attention. She was dancing like a song in fire and darting from the edge of one explosion to another. She was perfect in her performance. She needed to be. Anything less would be a trip to the ER, or worse.

She had on a Chinese black silk *cheongsam dress* with golden brocade highlights. A slit ran all of the way up her left thigh, her silky black hair ran all the way down to meet it. She held her high heels in her left hand and tried to protect her head with her right.

Nalu, instinctively and with no forethought of any kind, snagged her on the way past, reeling her into the shelter that he, Akina and Jesse commandeered. He grabbed her and swung her to the shelter of his arms just as twin rolls of 1,000 landed where she was going to be and lit up all around them with fire and concussions of doom.

In that moment, in that firelight and in those deafening explosions charring the sidewalks and road before them, they locked eyes. She saw him as her Hawaiian Superman; he saw her brilliant electric green eyes, and from that exact moment in time, things changed for both of them. *Auld Lang Syne* was being sung somewhere. Fireworks hit a maximum crescendo and, on the very last minute of 1976, Nalu and his mystery girl found each other – making it the best year ever for at least two people on planet Earth.

Jesse and Akina saw them together, sighed to each other, and sprinted for Duke's. Not so lucky in love but going to have fun amid the ongoing celebration just the same.

* * * * * * *

DIAMOND HEAD, ISLAND OF OAHU

On January 1st, 1977 at 4:15 p.m., The Boys were well into the first Maui Hold–Em game of the year. By then, only Nalu and William were left standing. Everybody else didn't have the cards, committed poker suicide by choice and by hangover, or had simply been vanquished by luck of the deal.

William, trying to direct attention from his weaker chip count, "Heard you found a babe last night – literally flew into your arms. " While flipping the first three cards for 'the flop'.

Nalu noticed William's micro expression of 'not joy' – and immediately bet most of what he saw in William's stack, he answered, "Her name is Mai Lin Chao originally from Hong Kong; she's *hapa* [mixed race]. Her father was British attaché and her mother was immigrant Chinese from Savannah Georgia of all places. Go figure, a Chinese girl with a British accent and twinges of southern belle. She looks Chinese and has brilliant green eyes – *unbelievable!*"

William, foolishly, matched the bet and then all in. With tremendous gusto he threw his shirt on the card table as was the prevailing Maui Hold-Em rule and the custom. He did it with great flare.

The 'turn' came with an ace of hearts; the 'river' card was a king of spades.

William leaped to his feet, threw down his newly found ace high straight, and went to put his shirt back on. Nalu calmly placed his hand over the stack, looked William in the eyes, and said, "Four twos! This one's mine – and thanks for the shirt! I'll use it for painting."

Nalu swept the pot as William moaned.

Everyone lost it, drank beer, and went back to the bowl game on T.V. The card game was just a reason to get together and pass around some tip money. It seemed it was almost impossible to win twice in a row with this crew.

But, for William, he was proving it was possible to lose time after time. He was down four flight coupons, fifty bucks and his favorite t-shirt, and that sucked. He trotted upstairs to find a new favorite t-shirt and get back to the bowl game with everyone else.

Nalu walked into the kitchen, grabbed the wall phone and called to see if Mai [graceful, elegance, gorgeous] was available for an early dinner. After all, *The Boys* were buying!

25

Schedules Of Joy

Late in the morning, on Haiwiki Ranch, the mid-morning sun finally burned through the cloud's misty layers and started turning the dew to vapors, making everything soft shades of white. It was a momentary affliction; for the crystal blue skies would appear and then dominate the remainder of the day in short order.

Mrs. Kealoha – coming back from the milk and bread run to Hawi Town below – stopped and got the day's mail. That's when she noticed the postcard wedged into the back of the ranch's jumbo mailbox built decades earlier. She thought, a good painting would do this old thing a service, or better yet, maybe Father could build a new one; it was high time.

She looked at the postcard, which had been trapped and unnoticed for way too long. Dog-eared and trashed it was looking rough. She thought, Who on Earth would send us a Hawaiian postcard? Then she took a good look at the front and the photo of a strange bay which had no caption and that it was postmarked from Ngerulmud, Melekcok State, Republic of Palau.

She read it to herself while sitting at the mailbox pull off, totally intrigued by this point in time, it said:

Dearest Ohana,

I am currently at Namai Bay visiting a long lost sister who needed a bit of encouragement. Hope your family had the most wonderful Christmas and may the coming year be a blessing in every way. I may be gone longer than anticipated for it seems that GOD alone knows my schedule.

Such is life when you rely on HIM for both navigation and wind power!

Please accept my heartfelt thanks for taking care of my Arabian that I miss so much; I hope that your 'gelding' enjoys his new love on the prettiest ranch upon the Kohala Mountains.

With much Aloha,

Grace

The date on the postmark was smudged beyond recognition, but the photo was of lime green mushroom islands sitting in a bay of deep clear blues and pockets of exposed sandbars. Ahhhhh … Micronesia, maybe some day, she thought, but knew that it probably wouldn't be in this lifetime.

Mrs. K. got a huge smile on her face, it appeared that any contact with Grace – even over vast reaches of distance and time – had that effect upon the human spirit. So nice to hear from her and this new information made it wonderful for the frolicking pair of inseparable horses that lingered into the ever-bluing skies above.

*   *   *   *   *   *   *

DEEP SOUTH PACIFIC, ISLAND NATION OF PALAU

Some weeks earlier, as Grace rounded the southern tip of Palau's tiny islets in various bays and inlets, she stopped to fish for an afternoon, catching many but keeping only one sixty pound ono. She grilled a little bit at sunset, salted some then crushed the salted fillets between two screens to sun dry for later. The remaining portions she gave to a group of children playing along the shoreline. They immediately ran back toward their homes on stilts, singing a new song about the 'Lady of Beauty' giving fish away!

Pulling anchor the following morning at high tide, she set sail for the downhill run toward the South China Sea – heading certain – destination unknown.

154

Epilogue

Songs Of Courage

Mr.Fujitani still had trouble sleeping through the night: many thoughts would race through his mind as he lay awake in bed. So many unusual events had transpired over the course of the previous months: the near elimination of his entire immediate family, their rescue by a mere boy whom he would have barely given notice to and would have expected a deep and reverent bow from. It rocked his perception of both the people around him and the spiritual nature of them, and himself, as well. Late every night, as the darkness invaded, he'd have whispers of calling and visions of places he'd never dreamed of. It confused him beyond belief, for it had become obvious at dwellings within his heart that he was being transported toward a destination unknown. At ever increasing speeds by an invisible force – truly more like an invisible hand – who, what, where, why? So many questions, and then this one overriding event. The 3:33 time phenomena actually made his short black hair stand up on the back of his neck, goose bumps race across his forearms, and everything else fade away as he pondered.

Then Mr. Kealoha-san read that verse out of his ancient Biblical text which gave an explanation he comprehended but wished to not understand.

Then the 'bells'! How on Earth had he been brought into their domain? Their enigma? Their energy? Their calling?

Their song from ages past?!

155

He looked tentatively at the clock, hoping for a different number, yet he watched it click from 3:32 a.m. to 3:33 a.m.. Forlornly he rolled over in his black silk pajamas and hugged his wife, then slept a few more hours until the dawn shook the good and bad alike awake all across Osaka Prefecture. Pushing them to race the race of human activity, scurrying to do what seemed so important, so needed yet so normally redundant and tedious for many souls across every level of Osaka's society, the high and the unmighty alike.

"Good morning, Mr.Fujitani-san" said the guards at the gate, the receptionist inside, the guards at the first inner doors and then the lab personnel working the 'Imperial Singing Bells' dilemma inside.

Once he'd gotten past all of the formal greetings from his staff and the less formal, but more heartfelt greetings, from the American scientist, he asked the question that had been forming very distinctly within.

"Dr. MIT, any progress on what this 'device' does? How do we activate it? What does it hold yet for us to discover?" said Mr. Fujitani, not just to the gentleman before him but to the whole team assembled around him.

"Just getting ready to perform the next experiment, this is Phase II – Experiment 201. We've tried various flow rates of water and intensities of light. We tried total changes and ranges of sounds projected at the bells and many combinations of all of these elements. To no real avail. Every time we perform the tests, the 'bells' 'sing' – but so far – no new 'song' or information has emerged. Yet, call it a deep-seated hunch, or guess if you prefer, I believe that the best   information is still right before us. We have switched tact with this next test, so please observe the clean room as we ramp up for it. Should be ready in a few minutes." Then he went back to calibrations on the makeshift controls wired before him.

Mr.Fujitani looked around him and walked over to Soni and Yurri, a few steps away, smiling he asked, "How are my favorite newlyweds, all is most wonderful I hope?"

Soni walked over and hugged him – most unusual for the Japanese. Yurri smiled and in his best Japanese said, "Good morning Mr. Fujitani-san. Wonderful to see you here! I think we may be on to something with this new phase of experiments ... ."

Mr. Fujitani looked at Soni with a bit of puzzled emotion darting across his eyes. Then, very uncharacteristically hugged her back. Some deep withheld stoic emotions were evaporating and opening his eyes to the brevity of life and its fragile nature.

Experiment 201 went live by first flowing ten gallons per minute of the Himalayan glacier water delivered as falling rain from spray nozzles above, light was turned to maximum, four Bose 901 speakers, set up North South East West, were activated playing a continuous Middle C at 100 decibels. Upon this combination of stimulation, the bells glowed deep-deep-deep indigo purple. Iridescence flooded the clean room with light and resonating with the matched pitch of the projected sound waves. 'Singing' was flooding the room all around as well.

All of this had been achieved in prior experiments, nothing new yet to be seen, but today's 'twist' was added as a small servomotor was spooled up and a clutch engaged slowly, spinning the bells on their axis by their common connector points in the middle. At exactly 1,000 rpms, everything erupted, as what had been a glow, now became a projection. An obvious projection cast upon the very space within the room, projected drops of light suspended at various levels and layers within the falling rain. Tremendous amounts of letters, words, phrases, pictures hung suspended in space before them. All was out of focus and was therefore indecipherable, yet there it was, success, even incomplete, was before them, a major breakthrough had occurred!

Every one of them stared, once more in awe, then as a team wildly broke into joyous shouts and spontaneous clapping.

After a short while, Dr. MIT, having made sure that the high-speed, high definition cameras had all been up and running to record the event, started to slowly power down the servomotors and bring the bells to a rest.

Dead silence betrayed the event that had just been witnessed by the diverse team for the first time in how many centuries – or for that matter – millennia?

At that exact moment, a muffled concussion and tremor shook the room, ductwork fell through newly formed cracks in the ceiling above, and everyone had bewildered looks on their faces, except for Yurri, who, without any hesitation launched into action.

Yurri scrambled the confused team and lab technicians to the back escape elevator that had been built for times such as this. The Keiretsu, having been survivors of the disaster known as WWII, had built at extreme expense, multi-layered security. But, even better yet, they had installed failsafe escape and evade mechanisms as well. Like this oneway elevator to the secret tunnel leading to an underground chamber beneath the manufacturing facility two blocks away. Known only to Mr. Fujitani and his closest confidents, Yurri being one. Secondly, the clean room had a false bottom floor that allowed the center section to drop into a time delayed vault far below. Encased in cement and rebar at thirty meters, it would be three days before the locks would be available to be activated for any reason and the 'bells' to be accessed.

Yurri shoved everyone into the elevator and hit the one-way descent button, placing Soni in her uncle's arms. He gave her a longing look of love, and then stepped back into the coming storm.

Someone had breached security! The concussion was a bomb being detonated via shaped charge, taking out the first level of defense. It was only a matter of seconds before the second charge breached the doors and allowed whoever was after the 'bells' into the lab complex. Yurri punched the drop button for the 'bells' descent to the vault below and waited with a large fire extinguisher for whoever rushed inside.

Yurri recited an ancient prayer handed down by one valiant warrior to another, through the annals of time, since before King David's reign, origin unknown: *"For my life is yours Lord, lead me where I must be. Time is too short, too precious to be anywhere else but exactly where You need and desire for me to dwell. Give me the strength to be the catalyst for the outcome you command. For I am Your's, my Lord, You are my King and there is no other. Thank You for blessing me with the courage that I will need. Amen."*

Yurri locked the fire extinguisher on and flipped it toward the door as he waited behind a reinforced concrete, load-bearing wall. It fogged everything just as the second explosion flashed!

The doors burst open!

And all hell came inside ... ...

* * * * * * *

* * * * * * *

The Epic Journey Continues:

Rain Falling On Bells

Book 1:

Fragments Of Truths

Rain Falling On Bells

Book 2:

Deep Blue Secrets

Rain Falling On Bells

Book 3:

Joy Dawn

Rain Falling On Bells

Book 4:

Couragous Dragonflies

Rain Falling On Bells

Book 5:

Brave Love

Also by Author:

The Gold Illusion

"Summer Rains"

&

The Leatherwood

A Historically Inaccurate Novel Gone Wondrously Astray

All Books May Be Purchased:

AMAZON BOOKS

&

CREATE SPACE

Made in the USA
Middletown, DE
13 March 2019